Frankenstein

The Legendary Gothic Science Fiction Novel

A Modern Translation

Adapted for the Contemporary Reader

Mary Shelley

Translated by Tim Zengerink

Table of Contents

Preface - Message to the Reader

What If You Could Help Rebuild the Greatest Library in Human History?

Thousands of years ago, the Library of Alexandria stood as the crown jewel of human achievement — a sanctuary where the collected wisdom of every known civilization was gathered, preserved, and shared freely.

And then, it was lost.

Through fire, conquest, and the slow erosion of time, humanity lost not just books — but ideas, dreams, discoveries, and stories that could have changed the world forever.

Today, the Library of Alexandria lives again — and you are invited to be a part of its restoration.

Our mission is simple yet profound:

To rebuild the greatest library the world has ever known, and to translate all timeless works into every language and dialect, so that no seeker of knowledge is ever left behind again.

By joining our movement to rebuild the modern Library of Alexandria, you become part of an unprecedented mission:

- **Unlimited Access to the Greatest Audiobooks & eBooks Ever Written:**

  Instantly explore thousands of legendary works—Plato, Shakespeare, Jane Austen, Leo Tolstoy, and countless more. All instantly available to read or listen, placing a complete literary universe at your fingertips.

- **Beautiful Paperback & Deluxe Editions at Printing Cost**

  Own any title as an elegant paperback, deluxe hardcover, or stunning collectible boxset—offered to you at true printing cost, delivered straight to your door. Build your personal Library of Alexandria, crafted for beauty, built for durability, and worthy of proud display.

- **Fresh Translations for Modern Readers—in Every Language & Dialect**

  Enjoy timeless masterpieces reimagined in clear, contemporary language—no more outdated phrases or obscure references. Alongside the original versions, we're tirelessly translating these classics into every language and dialect imaginable, ensuring accessibility and understanding across cultures and generations.

- **Join a Global Renaissance of Literature & Knowledge**

  You directly support expanding our library, publishing deluxe editions at true cost, translating works into all global languages, and bringing humanity's greatest stories to people everywhere. By joining today, you're not just preserving a legacy of masterpieces; you set in motion a powerful wave of literary accessibility.

Become a Torchbearer of Knowledge.

Join us for free now at **LibraryofAlexandria.com**

Together, we will ensure that the light of human wisdom never fades again.

With gratitude and a shared love of knowledge,

The Modern Library of Alexandria Team

Visit:

www.libraryofalexandria.com

Or scan the code below:

Introduction

A Monster Born of Imagination, Science, and Isolation

Frankenstein; or, The Modern Prometheus by Mary Shelley is much more than a simple horror tale—it is one of the most profound and visionary works of literature ever written. Conceived during a rainy summer in 1816, when Mary Shelley was barely eighteen, the novel emerged from a fateful gathering at Lake Geneva with some of the most brilliant minds of the Romantic era, including her future husband Percy Bysshe Shelley, Lord Byron, and John Polidori. It was during one of their evenings of storytelling that Lord Byron proposed a challenge: each guest should write a ghost story. From that dare, Mary Shelley would give the world a myth so resonant, so prescient, that it continues to shape how we think about science, ethics, identity, and the human condition.

Published anonymously in 1818 and later under her own name in the 1831 edition, Frankenstein tells the story of Victor Frankenstein, a young scientist who becomes obsessed with the secrets of life and death. Through an ambitious experiment, he manages to animate lifeless matter and creates a sentient being. But instead of celebrating his success, Victor is repulsed by his own creation and flees, setting into motion a tragic chain of events. The being—often mistakenly called Frankenstein—seeks connection and understanding but is met with fear, hatred, and violence. Rejected by his creator and by society, he turns vengeful and embarks on a journey of destruction.

On the surface, the novel is a chilling gothic tale about the dangers of overreaching ambition. But beneath the horror lies a web of complex philosophical and emotional questions. What is the responsibility of a creator to their creation? What defines humanity—our appearance, our emotions, or our moral choices? Is evil born or made? Shelley's work is astonishingly modern in its exploration of these issues. Even now, in a world where artificial intelligence, cloning, and genetic engineering push the boundaries of what is possible, the themes of Frankenstein remain urgently relevant.

Mary Shelley's literary achievement lies not only in the depth of her ideas but in the novel's intricate structure. Told through a series of nested narratives—letters from Captain Walton to his sister, Victor Frankenstein's confessional tale, and the creature's own moving account—the book offers multiple perspectives that challenge readers to see beyond the obvious. The monster is not simply a villain, and Victor is not simply a hero. Shelley leaves us in a moral gray zone, where judgment is suspended and empathy is demanded. This narrative layering also emphasizes isolation, a theme that haunts every character in the book. Walton is isolated at sea; Victor isolates himself in his quest for knowledge; the creature is isolated by his form and lack of companionship. The novel explores not just physical exile, but the existential loneliness that comes from being misunderstood or feared.

The Age of Enlightenment, Romanticism, and the Ethics of Creation

Frankenstein is deeply rooted in the intellectual ferment of the late 18th and early 19th centuries. Mary Shelley was the daughter of two of the era's greatest thinkers—William Godwin, a political philosopher, and Mary Wollstonecraft, a pioneering feminist author. Raised in an environment that encouraged rigorous thought and radical questioning, Shelley absorbed the ideals of the Enlightenment: reason, progress, and scientific inquiry. But she also inherited the emotional intensity and imagination of Romanticism. The result is a novel that embodies both movements—at once rational and emotional, scientific and sublime, hopeful and tragic.

Victor Frankenstein is the embodiment of Enlightenment ambition gone awry. Inspired by outdated alchemical texts and the new sciences of electricity and chemistry, he dreams of mastering life itself. His ambition reflects a belief in human mastery over nature, a hallmark of Enlightenment thinking. Yet Shelley's portrayal is far from celebratory. Victor's pursuit is obsessive and isolating. He ignores the moral implications of his work, and when he finally achieves his goal, he cannot bear the result. In this way, Shelley critiques not only the reckless pursuit of knowledge but the arrogance that often accompanies it.

The subtitle of the novel—The Modern Prometheus—underscores this cautionary message. In Greek mythology, Prometheus stole fire from the gods to give to humanity, an act of defiance that brought both enlightenment and punishment. Like Prometheus, Victor brings a forbidden gift to mankind—life from death—but suffers dearly for it. He is tormented by guilt, fear, and loss. His punishment is not divine wrath, but psychological disintegration and the destruction of everyone he loves. Shelley warns that the pursuit of godlike power, without compassion or foresight, will inevitably lead to ruin.

Yet the novel's most powerful ethical critique lies in its treatment of the creature. Made from dead flesh and brought to life, he is never given a name—a literary choice that signals his exclusion from society and identity. The creature begins life as a blank slate, curious and compassionate. He reads Paradise Lost, studies human behavior, and longs to be accepted. But repeated rejections turn his longing into hatred. His descent into violence is not a result of inherent evil, but of social alienation. Shelley asks us: who is the real monster—the creature, or the society that refuses to see his humanity?

This moral complexity is what makes Frankenstein so radical. Instead of a simple battle between good and evil, we see a tragedy rooted in misunderstanding, neglect, and unchecked ambition. The novel compels us to think about the ethical responsibilities of scientists, the rights of sentient beings, and the consequences of playing god. In an age where we create machines that can learn, modify genes, and extend human life, these questions are no longer theoretical. Shelley's vision has become a blueprint for modern debates about science, technology, and ethics.

Frankenstein's Enduring Power and Relevance

More than two hundred years after its publication, Frankenstein remains a cultural touchstone. The image of the monster—stitched together, grotesque, yet tragically human—has become an icon. But popular adaptations often simplify the story, turning the creature into a mute villain and Victor into a misguided hero. This modern translation restores the complexity of Shelley's original vision, updating the language for accessibility while preserving the novel's philosophical and emotional depth.

In this version, readers will encounter the novel as Mary Shelley intended: a work of staggering insight and emotional force. The characters' voices have been carefully preserved, and the narrative structure remains intact. What has changed is the language—now made more direct and fluid to suit today's readers. The goal of this modern adaptation is not to rewrite Shelley's masterpiece, but to open its doors to a broader audience. With updated prose, readers can fully engage with the novel's emotional resonance, moral dilemmas, and imaginative scope.

At its heart, Frankenstein is about what it means to be human. It is a meditation on birth and death, creation and abandonment, knowledge and ignorance, justice and vengeance. It explores the boundaries between self and other, science and soul, love and loss. These are themes that transcend time, place, and genre. Whether we are parents, teachers, creators, or citizens, we all bear some responsibility for what we bring into the world—and for how we treat those who are different from us.

The novel also offers a warning against hubris. In a world obsessed with progress, efficiency, and technological advancement, Frankenstein reminds us that without ethics, empathy, and humility, our creations can destroy us. The creature is not evil by nature; he is made monstrous by rejection. Victor is not a villain by intention; he becomes one through neglect. Their story is a tragedy, not of science, but of failed relationships and lost responsibility.

Reading Frankenstein today is not just an exercise in literary appreciation—it is a call to reflection. As we grapple with the moral dilemmas of our age, we would do well to remember the lessons Mary Shelley offered so long ago. Her novel is a mirror, showing us our fears, our hopes, and the responsibilities that come with creation. It challenges us to look past appearances, to think deeply about our choices, and to recognize the humanity even in those we fear or misunderstand.

This modern translation offers a chance to rediscover the brilliance of Mary Shelley's vision. Whether you are new to the novel or returning to it with fresh eyes, this edition is designed to draw you into the heart of the story—to feel the terror, the wonder, and the sorrow that lie at its core. Frankenstein is not just a story about monsters. It is a story about all of us—our dreams, our mistakes, and our desperate need to be seen and loved.

Letter 1

To Mrs. Saville, England

St. Petersburg, December 11th, 17—

You will be happy to hear that my journey has begun without any disasters, despite your worries about it. I arrived here yesterday, and the first thing I wanted to do was assure you, my dear sister, that I am safe and more confident than ever in the success of my mission.

I am already far north of London, and as I walk through the streets of St. Petersburg, I can feel the cold northern wind against my face. It sharpens my senses and fills me with excitement. Can you understand this feeling? This wind has come from the lands I am heading toward, giving me a taste of the icy world ahead. It fills me with even more determination.

People may say that the North Pole is nothing but ice and emptiness, but in my mind, I see it as a land of beauty and wonder. Imagine, Margaret, a place where the sun never truly sets, its golden light stretching across the sky at all hours. I trust the explorers who have gone before me when they say that, beyond the frozen wastelands, there may be lands no one has ever seen—places more incredible than anything discovered before. Who knows what mysteries exist in a land of endless daylight?

Perhaps I will uncover the secret behind the force that pulls the compass needle northward. Maybe I will be able to study the stars and planets in a way no one ever has before. Most of all, I will finally satisfy my burning curiosity by stepping onto a part of the world no human has ever set foot on. These dreams are enough to make me forget any fear of danger or death. Instead, I feel the same excitement a child feels when setting out on a small adventure.

Even if all of these ideas turn out to be wrong, I will still make an important contribution to the world. I might discover a faster sea route near the North Pole, saving months of travel for future explorers. Or I may unlock the mystery of magnetism, something that can only be studied in a place like this.

Thinking about these possibilities has calmed my nerves. Instead of worry, I feel a deep sense of purpose, and that fills me with peace. Nothing brings more stability to the mind than having a clear goal to focus on.

This journey has been my dream since childhood. You may remember how I used to read about explorers who tried to find a path through the icy seas of the North. Our Uncle Thomas had an entire library filled with books on the subject. Even though my formal education was limited, I loved reading. I spent day and night absorbed in these stories, and they only made me more regretful that my father's dying wish prevented me from becoming a sailor.

For a while, I gave up on that dream. When I first discovered poetry, I was completely enchanted by it. I even believed I might become a great poet myself. For a whole year, I lived in a fantasy world of my own making, imagining my name alongside Shakespeare and Homer. But you already know how that ended—my failure was painful.

At that same time, I inherited my cousin's fortune. With that, my thoughts returned to my childhood dream.

For the last six years, I have been preparing for this journey. I still remember the exact moment I dedicated myself to it.

I began by training my body to endure hardship. I joined whaling ships on several expeditions to the North Sea. I pushed myself to survive in the cold, to go without food or water, and to work with little sleep. I labored harder than the common sailors during the day and spent my nights studying mathematics, medicine, and the sciences that would help me as a navigator. Twice, I even took a job as a junior officer on a whaling ship in Greenland, and I did so well that my captain offered me a promotion. He begged me to stay, believing I was too valuable to lose. I admit, I felt proud of that.

Now, Margaret, after all this effort, don't I deserve to accomplish something great? I could have spent my life in comfort and luxury, but I chose adventure instead. Oh, how I wish someone would tell me I am right to do this! My courage is strong, but sometimes my hopes rise and fall, and I feel uncertain. This journey will be long and difficult. I will have to keep the spirits of my crew high, and at times, I will need to lift my own when doubt creeps in.

Right now is the best season to travel in Russia. The sleds glide smoothly over the snow, and the ride is pleasant—far better, in my opinion, than the jolting of an English stagecoach. The cold isn't unbearable if you are wrapped in furs, which I have already started wearing. But there is a big difference between walking around on the deck of a ship and sitting still for hours on end. Without movement, the cold can seep into your very bones. I have no desire to freeze to death on the road from St. Petersburg to Archangel.

In two or three weeks, I will leave for Archangel. Once I arrive, I will hire a ship, which can be arranged by paying for the owner's insurance. Then, I will gather my crew from among the experienced whalers there. I do not plan to set sail until June.

As for when I will return?

That, dear sister, is a question I cannot answer.

If I succeed, many months—perhaps even years—may pass before we see each other again. If I fail, you will see me much sooner... or never.

Farewell, my dear Margaret. May heaven bless you and keep me safe, so that I may return and show my gratitude for all your love and kindness.

Your devoted brother,

R. Walton

Letter 2

To Mrs. Saville, England

Archangel, March 28th, 17—

Time moves so slowly here, surrounded by nothing but ice and snow! Yet I have taken another step toward my goal. I have hired a ship and am now gathering my crew. The men I have found so far seem reliable and fearless.

But there is something I lack, something I have always wished for, and I feel its absence deeply—I have no friend, Margaret. If I succeed, there will be no one to share my joy. If I fail, there will be no one to comfort me. Of course, I can write down my thoughts, but that is not the same as sharing them with someone who truly understands.

I long for a companion—a man who would listen to me, someone whose eyes would reflect my own thoughts. You may think I am being dramatic, but I deeply feel this loneliness. I have no one around me who is both kind and brave, intelligent and open-minded, someone who could help guide me, approve of my plans, or correct my mistakes. How much better I would be with such a friend!

I know I tend to act too quickly and get frustrated by obstacles. But worse than that, I have always felt the disadvantage of my education. For the first fourteen years of my life, I ran wild, reading nothing but Uncle Thomas' books about voyages. At that age, I discovered poetry and fell in love with it. But it wasn't until much later that I realized how much I had missed by not learning other languages and expanding my knowledge earlier. Now, at twenty-eight, I feel less educated than many schoolboys half my age.

It's true that I have thought deeply and dreamed big, but my ideas lack structure. More than anything, I need a friend—someone wise enough not to dismiss me as foolish, yet kind enough to help guide my mind.

But there is no use complaining. I will not find such a friend on the vast ocean, nor here in Archangel, among sailors and merchants. And yet, even among these rough men, there are still glimpses of kindness.

For example, my lieutenant is incredibly brave and determined. He is obsessed with rising through the ranks, eager to make a name for himself. He is an Englishman, and though he has little education and holds onto many of his cultural and professional biases, he still possesses a noble heart. I met him years ago on a whaling ship, and when I found him unemployed here, I was able to recruit him for this journey.

The ship's captain is also an extraordinary man. He is known for his kindness and leads his crew with fairness rather than fear. His reputation for honesty and courage made me eager to hire him. Having grown up under your care, with gentleness and kindness around me, I have always disliked the harsh discipline common on ships. I never believed it was necessary. So when I heard of a captain who earned respect without cruelty, I felt fortunate to secure him.

I first heard about him in an unusual way. A woman, whose life was forever changed by his kindness, told me his story.

Years ago, he fell in love with a young Russian woman of modest wealth. After earning a large sum of money from prize winnings, he asked for her hand in marriage, and her father agreed. But when he went to see her before the wedding, he found her in tears. She threw herself at his feet and begged him to let her go. She confessed that she loved another man—one who was poor, and whom her father would never allow her to marry.

Instead of being angry, my captain reassured her. Then, after learning the name of her true love, he abandoned his pursuit.

He had already bought a farm where he planned to settle for the rest of his life. But instead of keeping it, he gave it to her lover—along with all the money he had left—to help the man build a future.

Then, he went to the girl's father and asked him to allow her to marry the man she truly loved. But the father refused, believing it would be dishonorable to break his promise to my captain. Seeing no other way, my captain left his home country and did not return until he heard that the woman had finally been allowed to marry the man she loved.

"What a noble man!" you must be thinking. And you are right. But despite his kindness, he is completely uneducated. He speaks very little, and there is a carelessness about him that, while making his actions even more remarkable, also makes it harder to fully connect with him.

Still, do not think that I regret my decision or that I am having second thoughts. My mind is set, as firmly as fate itself. I will only delay my voyage until the weather allows me to leave. This winter has been severe, but spring is arriving early, so I may be able to set sail sooner than expected.

I will not take reckless risks—you know me well enough to trust that I will be careful, especially when the lives of others are in my hands.

I can hardly put into words how I feel now that my journey is so close. It is impossible to explain the strange mix of excitement and fear that fills me as I prepare to depart. I am heading toward a land of ice and fog, to places no one has ever explored. But do not worry—I will not be like the doomed sailor in The Rime of the Ancient Mariner, cursed for killing an albatross.

You may smile at my reference, but I must confess something. I believe that my love for the unknown, my deep passion for adventure, comes from reading that poem by one of the greatest modern poets.

There is something within me that I do not fully understand.

I am a practical man—I work hard, I persevere, and I put in great effort. But beyond that, I have a love for the mysterious and a deep belief in the extraordinary. This longing for the unknown is woven into all of my dreams and ambitions. It is what drives me beyond the normal path of life, pushing me toward the wild seas and uncharted lands I am about to explore.

But let me turn to something closer to my heart.

Will I ever see you again, Margaret?

Will I return after crossing vast oceans, sailing back through the southern tip of Africa or America? I do not dare to hope for such success, yet I cannot bear to think of failure either.

For now, continue to write to me whenever you can. There may be moments on my journey when your letters will be the only thing keeping my spirits up.

I love you dearly. If you never hear from me again, please remember me with kindness.

Your devoted brother,

Robert Walton

Letter 3

To Mrs. Saville, England

July 7th, 17—

My dear sister,

I am writing this quickly to let you know that I am safe and making good progress on my journey. This letter will reach England with a merchant ship that is returning from Archangel. It is luckier than I am, as I may not see my homeland again for many years.

Still, my spirits are high. My crew is brave and determined, and they do not seem troubled by the sheets of ice floating past us—warnings of the dangers that lie ahead. We have already sailed far north, but since it is the height of summer, the weather is not as cold as I expected. It is nothing like England, of course, but the southern winds that push us toward our destination carry a surprising warmth that I did not anticipate.

So far, nothing remarkable has happened—at least nothing worth writing about. We have faced a few strong winds and even had a small leak, but these are such common problems for sailors that experienced navigators barely consider them worth mentioning. If these are the worst troubles we face on this voyage, I will be satisfied.

Farewell, my dear Margaret. Please know that for my sake, as well as yours, I will not take reckless risks. I will remain calm, persistent, and careful.

But I will succeed—why should I not? I have already come so far, charting a path through these unexplored waters, guided by the very stars above me. Why should I not continue forward across this wild but obedient sea? What can stop a determined heart and a strong will?

Forgive me, my emotions have carried me away. I must end this letter now.

May heaven bless you, my beloved sister.

R.W.

Letter 4

To Mrs. Saville, England.

August 5th, 17

Something very strange happened to us recently, and I feel the need to write it down, even though I will probably see you before this letter reaches you.

Last Monday, July 31st, our ship was nearly trapped in ice, which surrounded us on all sides, leaving barely enough space to stay afloat. The situation was dangerous, made worse by a thick fog, so we stopped moving and waited, hoping for a change in the weather.

Around two o'clock, the fog lifted, revealing an endless stretch of ice in every direction. Some of the crew groaned in despair, and I felt uneasy myself, but then something unexpected caught our attention. In the distance, about half a mile away, we saw a sled pulled by dogs, carrying a figure that looked like a man—except he was enormous, much taller than any normal person. We watched through our telescopes as he traveled quickly across the ice until he disappeared into the distance.

This sight shocked us completely. We were supposed to be hundreds of miles away from any land, yet this strange traveler suggested otherwise. However, with the ice blocking our way, we had no chance of following him, no matter how closely we had watched his path.

Two hours later, we heard the sound of waves beneath the ice, and by nightfall, the ice broke apart, freeing our ship. We chose to wait until morning to continue, fearing the large chunks of ice floating in the dark. I took the opportunity to get some rest.

At first light, I went on deck and found the crew gathered on one side of the ship, speaking to someone in the water. It turned out to be another sled, just like the one we had seen earlier, drifting toward us on a piece of ice. Only one dog had survived the journey, and inside the sled was a man—half-dead from the cold—whom the sailors were trying to convince to come aboard. Unlike the first traveler, he did not look wild or unfamiliar but was clearly a European.

As I stepped forward, the ship's captain assured him, "Our commander won't let you die out here."

The stranger turned to me and, despite his weak state, spoke in English, though with a foreign accent. "Before I board your ship," he asked, "can you tell me where you are headed?"

I was stunned by his question. Here was a man barely clinging to life, yet instead of seeking immediate rescue, he wanted to know our destination—as if nothing else mattered. Still, I answered that we were on a voyage of discovery toward the North Pole.

Hearing this, he seemed satisfied and finally agreed to come aboard. Margaret, I wish you could have seen him. You would have been as shocked as I was. His body was so thin and frozen from suffering that I have never seen a man in such a miserable state. We tried to take him to the cabin for warmth, but as soon as he left the fresh air, he fainted. We had to bring him back to the deck, revive him with brandy, and force him to drink a little. Once he showed signs of life, we wrapped him in blankets and placed him near the stove in the kitchen. Slowly, he recovered enough to eat a little soup, which helped him regain strength.

For two days, he barely spoke, and I feared his mind had been damaged by his suffering. When he was well enough, I moved him to my cabin and cared for him as much as I could. He is one of the most fascinating people I have ever met. His eyes often hold a wild or even mad expression, but at times, when someone shows him even the smallest kindness, his whole face softens into a look of warmth and gratitude. However, he mostly seems sad and hopeless, sometimes even clenching his teeth as if crushed by sorrow.

As he regained strength, the crew grew curious and wanted to question him about his journey, but I refused to let them overwhelm him. He needed rest more than anything. However, one day, the lieutenant asked why he had traveled so far across the ice with such an unusual sled.

At once, his expression darkened. "I was chasing someone," he replied.

"And was this person traveling the same way?"

"Yes."

"Then we may have seen him," the lieutenant said. "The day before we found you, we saw a man on a sled, pulled by dogs, crossing the ice."

This startled the stranger, and he asked countless questions about the direction the traveler had gone. Later, when we were alone, he told me, "I am sure I have sparked your curiosity, just as I have with the crew. But you are too kind to ask."

I answered, "I would never pressure you to share anything before you are ready."

He gave me a strange look. "And yet, you saved my life. You have brought me back from the edge of death."

Not long after, he asked whether I thought the other sled had been destroyed when the ice broke apart. I told him I could not be sure. The ice didn't crack until midnight, so the traveler might have reached safety before then, but there was no way to know for certain.

From that moment, the stranger seemed to regain a sense of purpose. He insisted on going up on deck, watching for any sign of the other sled. Since he was still too weak to endure the harsh cold, I convinced him to stay inside, promising that someone would keep watch for him and notify him if anything appeared.

That is everything I have written in my journal about this strange event so far. The stranger is slowly recovering but speaks little and seems uneasy around anyone except me. Still, despite his silence, his manners are so gentle that even the sailors, though they hardly interact with him, feel drawn to him. As for myself, I have grown to care for him like a brother. His sorrow fills me with sympathy, and I cannot help but wonder what he has suffered.

I once wrote to you, dear Margaret, that I would find no friend on this vast ocean. Yet now I have met a man whom I would have been proud to call my brother—had fate not broken his spirit.

I will continue writing about him when there are new developments to share.

August 13th, 17—.

Each day, I grow more attached to my guest. He amazes me with his wisdom and kindness, yet I also feel deep sorrow for him. How can someone so remarkable be suffering so much? He speaks with such intelligence and passion that his words seem carefully chosen, yet they flow naturally and effortlessly.

His health has improved a lot, and he now spends most of his time on deck, constantly watching for the sled that passed before his. Even though he is clearly troubled, he doesn't let his own pain stop him from showing interest in others. He often asks about my goals, and I have shared them openly with him. He listens carefully, considering every detail of my plans and offering thoughtful insights. His attention made it easy for me to speak freely, to express my burning ambition, and to declare that I would give up everything—my fortune, my life, even my dreams—just to achieve my mission. What was one life compared to the great knowledge I hoped to gain? What was one death if it meant controlling the forces of nature?

As I spoke, a deep sadness spread across his face. He tried to hide it at first, covering his eyes with his hands, but I saw tears slip through his fingers. A heavy sigh escaped his chest. Seeing his pain, my voice faltered, and I fell silent. Finally, he spoke in a strained voice: "Poor man! Are you caught in the same madness as me? Have you, too, tasted the same dangerous temptation? Listen to me—let me tell you my story, and you will turn away before it is too late."

His words filled me with intense curiosity, but his overwhelming grief drained what little strength he had left. He needed many hours of rest and calm conversation before he was ready to speak again.

When he regained control of his emotions, he seemed almost ashamed of how much they had overpowered him. Determined to push past his sorrow, he turned the conversation back to me, asking about my past. My story was short, but it brought up many thoughts and reflections. I spoke of my longing for a true friend, someone who truly understood me. I told him how I believed that life without such a connection felt empty.

"I understand," he answered. "We are incomplete beings, unfinished and flawed. Without a friend—someone wiser, kinder, and dearer than ourselves—to guide and support us, we can never reach our full potential. I once had such a friend. He was the best of all men, so I know what true friendship means. You still have hope, a future ahead of you. There is no reason for you to despair. But I... I have lost everything. I can never start over."

His face grew calm, but his sorrow remained, settled deep in his expression. His quiet grief touched me deeply. He said nothing more and soon withdrew to his cabin.

Even in his broken state, no one appreciates the beauty of nature more than he does. The sight of the endless sky, the open sea, and the wonders of this frozen land still seem to lift his spirit, even if only for a moment. He is a man who lives two lives—one filled with suffering and loss, the other an escape into a world of thought, where he rises above pain and sorrow like a spirit untouched by earthly troubles.

You might laugh at how much I admire this mysterious traveler, but I know you wouldn't if you saw him yourself. You have spent much of your life among books, away from the distractions of society, and that has made you more thoughtful, more able to recognize true greatness. Perhaps that is why I am struggling to define what makes him stand so far above any other man I have ever met. It is something beyond intelligence, beyond skill—it is an extraordinary ability to understand the world, to see deeper than others do. His mind is sharp, his judgment is quick and precise, and his words flow with a grace that captivates anyone who listens. Even his voice carries an almost musical quality, commanding attention and stirring emotions in a way that is impossible to ignore.

August 19th, 17—.

Yesterday, the stranger said to me, "Captain Walton, you can easily see that I have been through terrible suffering. At one point, I decided that I would never share my story with anyone, but you have changed my mind. You, like me, are searching for knowledge and wisdom, and I can only hope that your pursuit doesn't become a curse, as mine has. I'm not sure if telling you about my misfortunes will help you, but since you are following a path similar to mine, facing the same dangers that led to my downfall, maybe my story will serve as a warning. If you succeed, you may learn something valuable from it; if you fail, perhaps it will bring you comfort.

"What I am about to tell you will sound unbelievable. If we were in a more ordinary place, I might worry that you wouldn't believe me— or even laugh at my words. But here, in these remote and mysterious lands, you have already seen things that most people would consider impossible. I have no doubt that my story will prove itself true as you hear it."

I was eager to listen, grateful that he was willing to share something so personal. At the same time, I hated the thought of making him relive his pain. I wanted to hear his tale, not just out of curiosity, but also because I hoped that, in some way, I could help him. I told him how much I appreciated his trust.

He shook his head. "I thank you for your kindness, but it is useless. My fate is already decided, and nothing can change it. I am only waiting for one last event before I can finally rest. I know you want to stop me," he added, noticing my concern, "but you are mistaken, my friend—if I may call you that. Nothing can alter what is meant to happen. Listen to my story, and you will understand how my destiny is set in stone."

He then told me that he would begin his story the next day when I had time to listen properly. I was deeply grateful for this, and I promised to write down everything he told me, as closely to his own words as possible, every night when my duties allowed. If I was too busy, I would at least take notes. I am certain that this manuscript will bring you great interest, but for me, who has come to know him and hear his story directly from his lips, it will hold an even deeper meaning.

Even now, as I begin this task, I can still hear his strong, steady voice. I see the sorrow in his shining eyes and the way his thin hand moves as he speaks with passion. His face, though worn by suffering, glows with the fire of his spirit. Whatever his story may be, it must be as tragic as a powerful ship caught in a storm, wrecked beyond repair.

Chapter 1

I was born in Geneva, and my family is one of the most respected in the republic. For many years, my ancestors held important government positions, and my father also served in public office with great honor. He was well-known for his honesty and dedication to his work, spending much of his younger years focused on his duties. Because of this, he did not marry until later in life, when he finally became a husband and father.

The story of how he met my mother reflects his true character, and I feel compelled to share it. One of his closest friends, a merchant named Beaufort, had once been wealthy but lost everything due to a series of misfortunes. He was a proud man and could not bear to live in the same place where he had once been so successful, now reduced to poverty. After paying off his debts honorably, he moved with his daughter to the town of Lucerne, where they lived in isolation and hardship.

My father cared deeply for Beaufort and was heartbroken by his decision to disappear. He believed his friend's pride was a mistake, keeping him from accepting the help he desperately needed. Determined to find him and offer his support, my father searched tirelessly for months. Finally, after nearly a year, he discovered Beaufort's whereabouts and rushed to see him.

He found him living in a small, run-down house in a poor part of town. The sight that greeted him was heartbreaking. Beaufort had saved only a little money from his former wealth, just enough to survive for a short time. He had hoped to find work, but months passed with no success. Left with too much time to dwell on his misfortune, his sorrow deepened, and he soon fell into an illness that left him bedridden.

His daughter, Caroline, cared for him with incredible devotion, but she knew their situation was becoming desperate. Their small savings were almost gone, and with no other way to survive, she took up simple work—sewing, weaving straw, and doing anything she could to earn a little money. It was barely enough to keep them from starving.

For months, she struggled alone, watching her father's condition worsen. She spent every moment caring for him, leaving her with little time to earn money. In the tenth month, he passed away in her arms, leaving her completely alone in the world. Overcome with grief, she collapsed beside his coffin, crying, when my father entered the room. In that moment, he became her protector. After arranging for his friend's burial, he brought Caroline back to Geneva and placed her under the care of a relative. Two years later, she became his wife.

Though my parents had a significant age difference, their love for each other only grew stronger. My father believed that true love required deep respect and admiration. Perhaps, in his younger years, he had been disappointed by those he once cared for, which made him value true goodness even more. His love for my mother was not the blind devotion of an old man to a young wife, but rather a heartfelt admiration for her strength and kindness. He did everything he could to make her happy, protecting her from anything that might cause her distress, much like a gardener shielding a delicate flower from harsh winds.

The hardships she had endured had weakened her health and spirit, and my father was determined to help her recover. In the two years before they married, he slowly stepped away from public life, and after their wedding, they left for Italy. He hoped that traveling through this beautiful country would help her heal.

Their journey took them from Italy to Germany and France. I, their first child, was born in Naples and spent my early years traveling with them. For a long time, I was their only child, and they poured all their love into me. My mother's gentle affection and my father's warm smiles are among my earliest memories. I was their joy, their treasure, and most importantly, their child—the helpless little being they had brought into the world, whose future was shaped by their love and guidance. They took this responsibility seriously, and with all their devotion, they raised me with patience, kindness, and care. To me, every lesson felt like an adventure, every day filled with warmth and happiness.

For years, I was their only concern. My mother had always dreamed of having a daughter, but I remained their only child. When I was about five, they took a trip beyond Italy's borders and spent a week near Lake Como. My parents had generous hearts and often visited the homes of the poor, not just out of duty, but because my mother felt it was her purpose to help those in need. She never forgot her own struggles, and now that she had been saved, she wanted to do the same for others.

One day, while walking through a quiet valley, she noticed a small, run-down cottage that looked particularly sad and abandoned. Outside, several ragged children played, their thin faces showing signs of poverty. Their parents, a hardworking but exhausted couple, were struggling to provide for them.

Inside that home, however, there was one child who stood out from the others. While the other children had dark eyes and rough features, this girl was different. She was delicate and fair, her golden hair shining like a crown even in her tattered clothes. Her blue eyes were bright and clear, and her face was full of kindness and innocence. Anyone who looked at her would know she was special, almost as if she belonged to another world.

The woman who cared for the child noticed the way my mother gazed at her with admiration and quickly shared her story. The girl was not her daughter but the child of a nobleman from Milan. Her mother, who was German, had died giving birth to her. When she was just an infant, she had been placed in the care of this peasant family, who were in a much better situation at the time. They had only been married for a short while, and their first child had just been born.

The girl's father was one of those Italians deeply devoted to the dream of restoring his country's former glory. He fought for its freedom but became a victim of its struggles. No one knew for sure if he had died or if he was still locked away in an Austrian prison. His property was taken, and his daughter was left without family or wealth. She remained with her foster parents and grew up in their simple home, standing out among her surroundings like a bright, beautiful rose among thorny bushes.

When my father returned from Milan, he was surprised to find a child playing with me in the hallway of our villa. She was so delicate and beautiful that she seemed almost unreal, like a figure from a painting or a spirit from a dream. Her graceful movements were as light as a mountain deer. It did not take long for him to learn the reason for her presence. My mother had convinced her caretakers to let her take the child into our home. They loved her dearly, and her presence had been a joy to them, but they knew it would be wrong to keep her in poverty when she had been given a chance at a better life. After seeking guidance from their village priest, they agreed, and so Elizabeth Lavenza became part of our family. She was more than a sister to me—

she became my closest companion, sharing in all my joys and adventures.

Elizabeth was adored by everyone. The love and admiration she received from those around her filled me with both pride and happiness. The night before she came to live with us, my mother teased me, saying, "I have a special gift for Victor—he will receive it tomorrow." When the next day arrived, she introduced Elizabeth to me as that gift. Being just a child, I took her words literally and believed that Elizabeth truly belonged to me—someone to protect, love, and cherish forever. Every compliment given to her felt like a compliment to something that was mine. Though we called each other "cousin," there was no word that truly captured our bond. She was more than a sister, and in my heart, I believed that she would always be mine.

Chapter 2

Elizabeth and I grew up together, with less than a year between us. We never argued or had any kind of conflict. Our personalities were different, yet this only brought us closer. She was calm and thoughtful, while I was more passionate and eager to learn. She found joy in poetry and admired the beauty of the world around us—the towering mountains, the changing seasons, the peaceful winters, and the lively summers of our Swiss home. While she took in these wonders with quiet appreciation, I was driven to understand them. The world seemed full of mysteries, and I was determined to uncover them. From a young age, I was filled with curiosity and excitement whenever I learned something new about nature and its hidden laws.

When my younger brother was born, seven years after me, my parents decided to settle down for good in Geneva, ending their years of traveling. We had a house in the city, but we spent most of our time at our home on the eastern shore of Lake Geneva, in Belrive. My parents lived a quiet life, and I preferred it that way as well. I never sought out large groups of friends but instead formed deep connections with just a few people. One of them was Henry Clerval, the son of a Geneva merchant. Henry had a brilliant mind and a vivid imagination. He loved adventure and was drawn to stories of knights, heroes, and great battles. He wrote poems and began crafting tales of magic and bravery. He even tried to get us to perform plays and act out scenes from the legends of King Arthur, the knights of the Round Table, and the warriors who fought for the Holy Land.

Looking back, I don't believe anyone could have had a happier childhood than mine. My parents were kind and loving, not the type to control us harshly or impose strict rules just for the sake of authority. Instead, they created a home filled with joy. Whenever I spent time with other families, I realized how lucky I was, and this only deepened my love and gratitude toward them.

I had a strong personality, and my emotions were often intense, but rather than focusing my energy on childish things, I threw myself into learning. However, I wasn't interested in everything. I didn't care much for languages, politics, or government systems. What fascinated me were the mysteries of the universe. I wanted to understand the natural world, the forces that shaped life, and even the hidden nature of the human soul. My mind was always drawn to deeper questions, searching for knowledge that went beyond the surface of things.

Henry, on the other hand, was more focused on people. He was fascinated by the way they lived, the struggles they faced, and the greatness they could achieve. His dream was to become one of the noble figures in history, someone who would leave a lasting impact on the world.

And then there was Elizabeth. She was like the warm light that kept our home peaceful and loving. Her kindness was endless, and her presence filled our lives with joy. No matter how deep I got into my studies, or how serious I became, she was always there to soften my edges and remind me of life's gentler side. Clerval, too, was influenced by her goodness. Though he was naturally kind, it was Elizabeth who showed him that true greatness wasn't just about bravery and adventure—it was about doing good for others.

I take great pleasure in remembering my childhood, back when my thoughts were full of dreams of discovery and ambition, before sadness and tragedy darkened my life. Yet even as I reflect on those bright days, I recognize how they set the stage for the sorrow that would later consume me. Looking back, I can see how the passion that would come to control my life began in small, almost unnoticeable ways— like a tiny stream that grows into a raging river, eventually sweeping away everything in its path.

Science, or natural philosophy, shaped my destiny, and so I must explain how I became obsessed with it. When I was thirteen, my family took a short trip to the baths near Thonon. Bad weather forced us to stay inside for a day, and while waiting at the inn, I happened to pick up a book by Cornelius Agrippa. At first, I wasn't very interested, but as I kept reading, I became completely fascinated by his ideas. It felt like my mind had suddenly been opened to an entirely new world of possibilities. Excited, I rushed to show my father what I had discovered.

My father barely glanced at the book before dismissing it. "Ah, Cornelius Agrippa," he said. "Don't waste your time on this nonsense."

Had he taken the time to explain why Agrippa's ideas had been disproven, and how modern science had progressed far beyond them, I might have been convinced to put the book aside and return to more practical studies. Perhaps my life would have taken a completely different path. But because he dismissed it so quickly, I assumed he hadn't really read it and didn't understand its contents. Instead of being discouraged, I became even more eager to learn more.

When we returned home, the first thing I did was find more of Agrippa's works, followed by books from Paracelsus and Albertus Magnus. I read them obsessively, fascinated by the strange and wonderful ideas they contained. To me, these books were hidden treasures, secrets known only to a few.

Even though modern scientists had made incredible discoveries, their work never satisfied me. No matter how much I studied, I always felt like there was more to uncover, more hidden truths that had yet to be revealed. Sir Isaac Newton once described himself as a child picking up seashells on the shore of a vast, unexplored ocean. To my young mind, even the greatest scientists of my time seemed like beginners, still searching for the deeper mysteries of the world.

A simple farmer knew how to use the elements around him in practical ways, but even the most educated scientist knew little more. Science had uncovered some of nature's secrets, but much of it remained a mystery. Scientists could study the human body, take it apart, and name its different parts, but they still didn't fully understand how life worked. I had looked at the obstacles that kept people from unlocking nature's deepest secrets, and instead of being patient, I had become frustrated.

But then I found books written by men who claimed to have discovered more, and I believed everything they said. I followed their ideas without question and became their devoted student. It may seem strange that such beliefs still existed in the 18th century, but while I received a formal education in Geneva, I was mostly self-taught when it came to the subjects that fascinated me the most. My father was not a scientist, so I had to figure things out on my own, driven by my endless curiosity.

Guided by these new teachers, I threw myself into the search for the philosopher's stone and the elixir of life. Before long, my focus shifted entirely to the latter. I wasn't interested in wealth—what truly excited me was the idea of eliminating disease and making humans immune to anything but violent death. The possibility of such a discovery filled me with ambition.

But that wasn't the only thing I dreamed of. The books I read claimed that spirits and demons could be summoned, and I became obsessed with making that happen. When my attempts failed, I didn't doubt the process—I simply assumed that I was inexperienced and had made mistakes. For a time, I was lost in these outdated ideas, mixing together different theories that often contradicted each other. I was overwhelmed by a flood of confusing knowledge, guided only by my imagination and youthful reasoning, until one event changed my way of thinking forever.

When I was fifteen, my family had returned to our home near Belrive. One night, a powerful thunderstorm swept over us, coming from behind the Jura mountains. The thunder roared from every direction, shaking the sky with terrifying force. Instead of hiding, I watched with fascination, mesmerized by the storm's intensity. As I stood at the door, a bolt of lightning struck an old oak tree about twenty yards from our house. A bright flash of fire lit up the night, and when the light faded, the tree was gone. All that remained was a blackened stump.

The next morning, we went to examine the remains of the tree. It hadn't just been broken or burned—it had been completely destroyed. The wood had been stripped away in thin ribbons, as if the tree had been reduced to nothing in an instant. I had never seen such total destruction before.

I already knew the basics of electricity, but this event made me more curious. A scientist happened to be staying with us at the time, and seeing my interest, he explained his theories about electricity and galvanism. His words amazed me. The ideas he shared were unlike anything I had read before, and suddenly, the books that had once inspired me—those written by Cornelius Agrippa, Albertus Magnus, and Paracelsus—seemed unimportant. Yet, instead of feeling excited about this new knowledge, I felt strangely discouraged. It was as if I had realized, all at once, that no one could ever truly understand the mysteries of the universe. Everything I had been so passionate about now felt meaningless.

In that moment, my interests changed completely. I abandoned my studies of natural philosophy, deciding that it was a failed science that could never uncover real truth. I turned instead to mathematics, which seemed more solid and reliable. Numbers and formulas felt like they were built on a firm foundation, unlike the uncertain theories I had spent so much time chasing.

It's strange how our minds work, how small events can push us toward success or lead us to ruin. Looking back, this sudden shift in my interests feels almost like an act of fate—like a final warning, a last attempt to steer me away from disaster. When I left my old studies behind, I felt peaceful and content, as if I had escaped something dangerous. It was as if I had been given a chance to associate my past research with suffering and my new studies with happiness.

But even that was not enough to change my fate. No matter what I did, destiny was too strong. The course of my life had already been set, and nothing could stop the terrible future that awaited me.

Chapter 3

When I turned seventeen, my parents decided that I should continue my studies at the University of Ingolstadt. Until then, I had attended school in Geneva, but my father believed that experiencing different customs and environments would complete my education. My departure was set for an early date, but before I could leave, tragedy struck—an event that seemed to foreshadow the misfortunes that would follow in my life.

Elizabeth fell ill with scarlet fever, and her condition was severe. She was in great danger, and many urged my mother to stay away to protect herself from infection. At first, she listened to our pleas, but as Elizabeth's condition worsened, she could no longer stand by and do nothing. She stayed by Elizabeth's bedside, caring for her day and night. Thanks to her devoted care, Elizabeth recovered—but the cost was devastating. My mother fell ill soon after, and her symptoms were far more alarming. The expressions of her doctors made it clear that they feared the worst.

Even on her deathbed, she remained strong and kind. She took Elizabeth's hand and mine, bringing them together. "My children," she said, "I had always hoped to see the two of you united. That thought brings me peace, and I know it will comfort your father as well. My dear Elizabeth, you must take my place and care for my younger children. I do not want to leave you all behind, but I must accept my fate. I will try to meet it with courage, and I hold onto the hope that we will see each other again in another world."

She passed away gently, and even in death, her face showed love and warmth. It is impossible to describe the emptiness left behind when someone so dear is suddenly gone. At first, the mind refuses to believe that the person you saw every day, whose presence was as natural as your own, could truly be gone forever. The light in their eyes, the sound of their voice—things so familiar—are suddenly lost, never to return. In the first days, grief is overwhelming, but as time passes, the reality sinks in, and the pain becomes even sharper. But who hasn't experienced such a loss? Who has not had someone taken from them by death? Why describe a sorrow that is universal, one that everyone will face at some point? Eventually, grief becomes something we hold onto rather than something that consumes us. And even though smiling again may feel wrong at first, life continues. My mother was gone, but we still had responsibilities to fulfill. We had to move forward, grateful for the loved ones we still had.

Because of my mother's passing, my departure for Ingolstadt was delayed, but eventually, it was decided that I should leave as planned. I convinced my father to give me a few more weeks at home. It felt wrong to leave so soon after such a loss, as if I were abandoning the quiet, grieving house to throw myself into a new life. I had never known real sorrow before, and it unsettled me. More than anything, I wanted to stay until Elizabeth found some comfort.

Despite her own grief, Elizabeth devoted herself to helping the rest of us heal. She took on her new role with quiet strength, caring for my father and my younger brothers with unwavering kindness. She was never more wonderful than in those days, bringing light back into our home with her warm smile and gentle presence. She hid her own sorrow to help ease ours.

Finally, the day of my departure arrived. Clerval spent my last evening at home with us. He had tried to convince his father to let him come with me to study, but his efforts were in vain. His father, a strict businessman, believed education was a waste of time and would only lead to failure. Henry said little about his disappointment, but I could see in his eyes that he was determined not to let his dreams slip away. He refused to be trapped in the life his father had planned for him.

That night, we stayed up late, unable to bring ourselves to say goodbye. Even when we finally parted, pretending to go to sleep, I knew we were only fooling ourselves. The next morning, as I stepped outside to leave, I found them all waiting for me—my father to give me his blessing, Clerval to grasp my hand one last time, and Elizabeth to remind me to write often. She fussed over me, making sure everything was in order before I left, just as she had always done when we were children.

I climbed into the carriage, and as it pulled away, I was filled with sadness. I had always been surrounded by loving companions, people who shared in each other's happiness. Now, for the first time, I was completely alone. At the university, I would have to make my own way, form new friendships, and rely on myself. My life had been quiet and sheltered, and because of this, I dreaded meeting strangers. I loved my father, my brothers, Elizabeth, and Clerval—these were the people I had always known, the ones who made up my world. I felt unprepared to step into the unknown.

These thoughts weighed on me at the start of my journey, but as I traveled, my mood shifted. My old excitement returned, and I was filled with anticipation. I had long dreamed of seeing the world beyond my home, of gaining knowledge and making something of myself. Now, that dream was becoming reality, and I knew it would be foolish to regret it.

The journey to Ingolstadt was long and exhausting, giving me plenty of time to reflect on everything that had happened. At last, I caught sight of the town's tall, white steeple. When I arrived, I was shown to my room, where I was left alone to spend the evening as I pleased.

The next morning, I delivered my letters of introduction and visited some of the university's most respected professors. By chance—or perhaps, by some cruel fate that had controlled my life ever since I unwillingly left home—I first met Professor Krempe, who taught natural philosophy. He was a rough and unpolished man, but he was deeply knowledgeable in his field. He questioned me about my studies, asking what I had learned in different branches of science. I answered casually, almost dismissively, mentioning that I had spent most of my time reading the works of ancient alchemists.

He stared at me in disbelief. "You've really wasted your time studying that nonsense?" he asked.

I admitted that I had.

"Every single minute you spent on those books was completely wasted," he said with growing intensity. "You've filled your head with outdated ideas and useless names! Tell me, where have you been living that no one bothered to tell you these ridiculous theories were disproven centuries ago? I can't believe that, in this modern age, I've met a student of Albertus Magnus and Paracelsus. My dear boy, you need to start over from the beginning."

With that, he quickly wrote down a list of books on natural philosophy and handed it to me, telling me to get copies for my studies. He then informed me that he would soon begin a lecture series on natural philosophy and that another professor, M. Waldman, would be lecturing on chemistry on alternating days.

I left the meeting without feeling disappointed. In truth, I had already begun to doubt the alchemists I had once admired, and Krempe only confirmed what I had long suspected. However, his rude manner and unappealing personality did nothing to inspire me. He was short and gruff, and I found him unlikable. Because of this, I had no motivation to take up the studies he so forcefully encouraged.

Looking back, I can now see why I had been drawn to the alchemists in my younger years. As a child, I was not satisfied with the careful and limited promises of modern science. Without a real guide, I had followed a strange and confused path, looking backward rather than forward, trading the discoveries of recent scientists for the dreams of long-forgotten alchemists. I had once admired the old philosophers because they aimed for greatness—seeking eternal life, unlimited power, and control over the elements. Even if their ideas were unrealistic, they had a boldness that fascinated me. Modern science, on the other hand, seemed narrow and uninspiring. Scientists no longer dreamed of grand discoveries; instead, they were focused on proving what was impossible. I had once believed I would have to trade my limitless ambitions for dull facts.

These thoughts occupied my mind during my first few days at Ingolstadt, which I mostly spent getting familiar with the town and meeting important people. When the following week arrived, I recalled what Krempe had said about the lectures. Though I refused to sit through a lecture by such an arrogant man, I remembered his mention of Professor Waldman, whom I had not yet met.

Out of curiosity—and, admittedly, because I had nothing else to do—I decided to attend one of Waldman's lectures. As I entered the lecture hall, the professor arrived shortly after. He was nothing like Krempe. Waldman appeared to be about fifty years old, with a kind and intelligent expression. His hair was mostly dark, though strands of gray lined his temples. He was short but carried himself with confidence, and his voice was the most pleasant I had ever heard.

He began by giving an overview of chemistry's history, passionately naming the great minds who had contributed to its development. Then, he briefly explained the current state of the science and broke down some of its basic concepts. After demonstrating a few simple experiments, he ended with a speech that I will never forget:

"The early scientists promised the impossible, yet achieved nothing. Today's scientists promise little, but what they accomplish is extraordinary. They no longer believe that metals can be transformed or that an elixir of life exists—but what they have discovered is even more incredible. These modern researchers, whose hands may seem made only to work in labs and whose eyes are fixed on microscopes and test tubes, have uncovered nature's deepest secrets. They have ventured into the unseen forces that shape our world. They have explored the heavens, uncovered the mysteries of blood circulation, and explained the very air we breathe. They have gained immense knowledge and nearly unlimited power. They can command lightning, imitate the force of earthquakes, and even reveal the invisible."

Those were the professor's words—or rather, the words of fate itself, spoken to bring about my downfall. As he continued, I felt as though my very soul was wrestling with an unseen force. His words struck something deep within me, awakening a passion that quickly took hold of my entire being. Thought after thought filled my mind, until I was left with a single purpose. So much has already been achieved, I thought. But I will accomplish far more. I will follow the paths already laid before me, yet I will go further, discovering new powers and uncovering the greatest mysteries of creation.

That night, I could not sleep. My thoughts were in chaos, burning with energy I could not control. I knew that eventually, order would come from this storm of ideas, but I had no power to calm it myself. As the morning light crept through my window, exhaustion finally overtook me, and I slept. When I awoke, the emotions of the previous night felt like a dream, but one thing remained clear: I had made up my mind. I would return to my old studies and dedicate myself fully to science, convinced that I had a natural gift for it.

Later that day, I visited Professor Waldman. In private, he was even more kind and approachable than he had been during his lecture. While he had carried himself with dignity before his students, in his own home, he was warm and welcoming. I told him about my past studies, much as I had told his colleague. He listened patiently, smiling when I mentioned names like Cornelius Agrippa and Paracelsus, but unlike Professor Krempe, he showed no scorn.

"These men," he said, "were pioneers in their time. Their tireless efforts paved the way for the discoveries of modern scientists. Though their theories were often misguided, their work helped uncover knowledge that might have otherwise remained hidden. It is because of them that today's philosophers have been able to organize and classify facts in a more structured way. The work of brilliant minds, even when flawed, almost always leads to some benefit for humanity."

I listened carefully, appreciating the fairness in his words. Unlike Krempe, he did not dismiss the past entirely but recognized its role in shaping modern science. His reasonable and open-minded approach eased my earlier doubts. I told him that his lecture had changed my view of modern chemists and that I was now ready to pursue my studies seriously. I spoke carefully, showing him the respect a student owes his teacher, yet I held back the enthusiasm burning inside me. My lack of experience in the world made me cautious, and I feared appearing too eager.

I then asked him for guidance on which books to study.

"I am pleased," said Professor Waldman, "to have gained a student. If you work as hard as I expect, I have no doubt that you will succeed. Chemistry has seen the greatest advancements in all of natural philosophy, which is why I have devoted myself to it. However, a true scientist must not focus on just one subject. A person who studies chemistry alone will never be great. If you truly wish to become a man of science and not just an experimenter, you must study all branches of natural philosophy, including mathematics."

He then took me into his laboratory, showing me his equipment and explaining how each instrument worked. He guided me on what materials I should acquire and even promised to let me use his own tools once I had gained enough experience to handle them properly. Finally, he gave me the list of books I had requested, and I thanked him before leaving.

That day was one I would never forget. It marked the moment my fate was sealed.

Chapter 4

From that day on, I devoted myself almost entirely to natural philosophy, with a special focus on chemistry in its broadest sense. I eagerly read the works of modern scientists, filled with brilliant ideas and careful analysis. I attended every lecture and made an effort to connect with the leading scholars at the university. Even Professor Krempe, despite his harsh appearance and gruff manners, proved to be highly knowledgeable and full of valuable insights. But it was in Professor Waldman that I found a true mentor. He never spoke with arrogance or acted superior, and his explanations were always clear and engaging. He had a way of making even the most difficult subjects easy to understand, guiding me along the path of knowledge with patience and encouragement.

At first, my studies lacked focus, but as time went on, my dedication grew stronger. Soon, I was so engrossed in my work that I would often stay in the laboratory until the night faded into morning. My rapid progress astonished my fellow students, and even the professors took notice. Professor Krempe would occasionally tease me about my earlier fascination with alchemy, while Professor Waldman openly expressed his pride in my achievements.

Two years passed this way. I was so deeply invested in my work that I never returned home to Geneva, completely absorbed in my pursuit of discovery. Science has a unique power to captivate the mind—unlike other fields of study, where once you reach a certain point, there is little left to uncover, science is endless. Every discovery leads to another, and the deeper you go, the more there is to explore. A person of average intelligence who dedicates themselves fully to a single pursuit will undoubtedly become skilled in it. Because I was so focused on one goal, I advanced quickly. By the end of two years, I had even developed improvements for certain chemical instruments, which earned me recognition and respect at the university.

At that point, I had learned as much as I could from the professors at Ingolstadt. I had mastered both the theory and practical aspects of natural philosophy, and it seemed that staying there any longer would not benefit my education. I began to think about returning home to my family, but then something happened that changed everything.

I had always been fascinated by the human body, as well as all living creatures. I often wondered, What is the source of life? It was a bold question, one that had always been surrounded by mystery. Yet I believed that so many discoveries lay just beyond our reach, if only we had the courage and determination to seek them out. The more I thought about it, the more determined I became to study the science of life itself.

This was not an easy field of study. In order to understand life, I first had to study death. I began learning about anatomy, but that alone was not enough. I needed to see, firsthand, how the body decays over time. My father had raised me to be rational and unafraid of superstition. I had never trembled at ghost stories or feared the dark. To me, a graveyard was nothing more than a place where lifeless bodies were laid to rest—bodies that had once been strong and beautiful but had now become food for worms.

Now, I had to examine that process up close. I spent days and nights in burial vaults and charnel houses, studying the slow decay of the human form. I forced myself to look at sights that would disturb most people. I saw how the body, once full of life, gradually broke down. The brightness of a person's eyes, the intelligence of their mind—all of it was lost to time. I studied these changes carefully, analyzing every stage of the transition from life to death, and from death to decay.

Then, from the depths of this darkness, a sudden realization came to me—one so astonishing, yet so simple, that I could hardly believe it had not been discovered before. The idea was so overwhelming that I felt dizzy thinking about its implications. It seemed impossible that among all the great scientists who had explored this subject, I alone had uncovered such a profound truth.

I must make it clear: I was not imagining things or caught in some mad dream. What I had discovered was as real and undeniable as the sun shining in the sky. Some might call it a miracle, but I had reached this knowledge step by step, through logic and relentless effort. After countless hours of exhausting work and research, I had uncovered the secret of life itself. More than that—I had found a way to bring lifeless matter back to life.

The excitement I first felt after my discovery quickly turned into pure joy. After so much hard work and struggle, finally reaching the goal I had dreamed of felt like the greatest reward. But the discovery was so overwhelming that I barely remembered the steps that had led me there—all I could see was the result. The knowledge that the greatest minds in history had sought for centuries was now in my hands.

However, it wasn't as if everything suddenly became clear in an instant. My discovery didn't complete my work—it only gave me the direction I needed to continue. It was like finding a tiny glimmer of light in total darkness, just enough to guide me forward but not enough to reveal everything at once.

I can see the curiosity and hope in your eyes, my friend. You want to know the secret I uncovered. But I cannot share it. Be patient, and by the end of my story, you will understand why. I refuse to lead you down the same reckless path I once took—a path that only leads to misery. Learn from me, not just from my words but from my mistakes. There is danger in gaining too much knowledge. A person who believes their small town is the entire world may be happier than one who tries to surpass the limits of human nature.

Once I realized the incredible power I had uncovered, I hesitated. How should I use it? I had learned how to bring life to lifeless matter, but building a body capable of receiving that life—one with all the complex systems of muscles, veins, and nerves—was still an incredibly difficult task. At first, I wasn't sure whether I should create something as complex as a human or a simpler creature. But my excitement and confidence in my discovery made me believe I could achieve something truly great. The materials I had available seemed insufficient for such a huge task, but I was certain I would succeed in the end. I prepared myself for failure after failure, knowing that my first attempt might not be perfect. Still, science and technology were improving every day, and I believed that even if I did not succeed immediately, my work would lay the foundation for future breakthroughs. The complexity of my goal did not scare me—it only made me more determined.

And so, with these thoughts, I began the creation of a human being. The small details of the human body made the work slow and difficult, so I decided to make my creation much larger than a normal person— about eight feet tall and built in proportion. Once I had made this decision, I spent months gathering materials and carefully preparing.

No words can fully explain the emotions that drove me forward, pushing me like a storm in the early excitement of success. I felt as though I was about to break through the limits of life and death, bringing a new kind of light to the world. I imagined that a new species of beings would one day exist because of me, and they would see me as their creator, grateful for the life I had given them. No father would ever be as important to his children as I would be to them. And as I pursued these thoughts, another idea took hold—I wondered if, in time, I could go even further. If I could bring life to something that had never lived before, perhaps I could also find a way to restore life to the dead.

These ideas gave me strength and kept me motivated, even as I exhausted myself with my work. I became pale and thin, shutting myself away from the outside world, focusing only on my goal. Many times, I thought I was about to succeed, only to have something go wrong. But no matter how many times I failed, I convinced myself that the answer was just within reach. The knowledge I had—the secret I alone possessed—was the only thing that kept me going. Night after night, I worked without rest, chasing nature's hidden truths.

But the work was horrifying. I spent countless hours in dark, damp graveyards, collecting bones and studying the secrets of the human body. I dissected both the dead and the living in my desperate search for answers. Thinking back on it now, my body trembles and my vision blurs, but at the time, I felt no fear or hesitation. I was completely consumed by my obsession. Nothing else mattered. I had lost all sense of the world around me—my entire existence had narrowed to this single pursuit.

My workshop was a small, isolated room at the top of my house, separated from the rest of the living space by a long hallway and staircase. There, surrounded by the remains of my grim work, I spent endless days and nights focused on every detail of my creation. I took materials from dissecting rooms and slaughterhouses, and though I often felt sickened by my own actions, I could not stop. My obsession only grew stronger, pushing me closer and closer to my goal.

The summer months passed as I remained completely focused on my work. It was a beautiful season—fields were full of crops, and the vineyards were richer than ever—but I hardly noticed. I had become so absorbed in my project that I was blind to the world around me. In the same way, I had also forgotten about my family and friends, who were miles away and whom I had not seen in a long time. I knew my silence worried them. I could still hear my father's words in my mind: "As long as you are happy and doing well, you will think of us and write to us. If you stop writing, I will take it as a sign that you are neglecting your other responsibilities as well."

I understood how he must have felt, but I couldn't bring myself to step away from my work. It had taken over my mind so completely that I ignored everything else—even though I found parts of it disgusting. I kept telling myself that I would return to my loved ones and all my usual habits once I had finished my great task. Nothing else seemed to matter until then.

At the time, I believed my father would be wrong to think I was at fault. But looking back, I see now that he had every reason to be concerned. A person striving for perfection should keep a calm and steady mind, never letting ambition or fleeting desires disturb their peace. I don't believe that the pursuit of knowledge is an exception. If studying something makes a person lose touch with their loved ones and takes away their appreciation for the simple joys of life, then it is not a worthy pursuit. If this rule had been followed throughout history, perhaps Greece would never have been conquered, Caesar would not have turned against his own country, America would have been discovered more gradually, and the civilizations of Mexico and Peru might not have been destroyed.

But I realize I am getting lost in these thoughts, and your expression reminds me to continue my story.

My father never scolded me in his letters. Instead, he simply asked more detailed questions about my studies, trying to understand why I had become so distant. While I worked, the seasons changed—winter, then spring, then summer again—but I no longer paid attention to the beauty of nature. I didn't notice the blooming flowers or the fresh green leaves, things that had once brought me great joy. My mind was too consumed by my work. By the time the leaves began to wither in the fall, I was nearing the end of my project. With each passing day, I saw more proof that I had succeeded.

But my excitement was mixed with anxiety. I no longer felt like a passionate scientist but rather like a prisoner, forced to work under terrible conditions. My health suffered greatly. Every night, I felt feverish, and I became so nervous that even the sound of a falling leaf would startle me. I avoided people as if I were hiding some terrible crime. Sometimes, I looked at myself in the mirror and barely recognized what I had become. But the only thing that kept me going was the belief that it would soon be over.

I told myself that once my work was finished, I would finally rest. I imagined that exercise and fresh air would heal me, that amusement and relaxation would restore my mind. I promised myself that as soon as my creation was complete, I would return to a normal life.

Chapter 5

On a cold and miserable November night, my work finally came to an end. My hands shook with anxiety as I gathered the tools I needed to bring life to the lifeless form lying before me. It was past midnight, and the rain beat heavily against the windows. My candle was nearly burned out, casting only a faint glow in the dark room. Then, in that dim light, I saw it—the creature's dull yellow eyes flickered open. Its chest rose and fell with heavy, uneven breaths, and its limbs twitched violently.

How can I even begin to describe the horror of that moment? I had worked tirelessly for nearly two years, carefully crafting every part of its body. I had chosen its features, believing I was creating something beautiful. Beautiful! Great God, how wrong I had been! Its yellow skin barely covered the muscles and veins beneath. Long black hair flowed from its head, and its white teeth gleamed—but these only made the rest of its face more disturbing. Its watery, colorless eyes blended into their pale sockets, its skin was tight and shriveled, and its thin black lips only added to the horror of its appearance.

Human emotions change faster than anything else in life. I had sacrificed everything for this moment—my health, my sleep, my sanity—all to give life to a body that had never lived. I had wanted it more than anything, chasing this dream with obsessive passion. But the moment I succeeded, my excitement vanished. All I felt was pure horror and disgust. I couldn't stand to look at the thing I had created. Overwhelmed, I ran from the room and paced my chamber, unable to rest. My mind was in complete turmoil. Eventually, exhaustion overtook me, and I collapsed onto my bed, still fully dressed, hoping for just a few moments of relief.

But sleep brought no peace. My dreams were wild and terrifying. I saw Elizabeth, full of life and happiness, walking through the streets of Ingolstadt. Overcome with joy, I embraced her. But as soon as I kissed her, her lips turned cold and pale, drained of life. Her face changed, and suddenly, I was holding the corpse of my dead mother. A burial shroud wrapped around her lifeless body, and I saw worms crawling through the folds of the cloth.

I woke up with a gasp, drenched in sweat, my body shaking violently. My teeth chattered, and I felt a chill deep in my bones. Then, in the weak yellow light of the moon shining through the window, I saw it—him. The miserable thing I had created.

He stood by my bed, pulling back the curtain. His hollow eyes stared at me. His mouth opened, and a low, garbled sound came from his throat. His face twisted into something that might have been a grin, but it was monstrous. One of his hands reached out toward me, as if trying to stop me from leaving.

I didn't wait to see what he would do next. Panic took over, and I bolted from the room, running down the stairs without looking back. I rushed outside and into the courtyard of the house. There, I spent the rest of the night pacing frantically, jumping at every sound, terrified that the creature would come after me.

No human being could endure the horror of that face. Even a reanimated corpse from an ancient tomb would not look as horrifying as the thing I had given life to. I had seen it before it was finished, and even then, it had been hideous. But now that it could move, now that its muscles and joints worked, it had become something truly nightmarish—something so terrible that even the darkest imagination could not have dreamed it.

That night was a nightmare. My heart raced so fast and so hard that I could feel my pulse pounding in every part of my body. Other times, I felt so weak that I thought I might collapse. But worse than the horror I felt was the crushing disappointment. My dreams had kept me going for so long, filling my mind with endless possibilities. Now, those same dreams had turned into a living nightmare. The change had been so sudden, so complete, that I could hardly grasp the reality of it.

Morning finally came, but it brought no relief. The sky was dark and full of rain, and as I looked up with tired, aching eyes, I saw the white steeple and clock tower of Ingolstadt. It was six o'clock. The porter opened the gates of the courtyard, and I stepped out onto the streets, walking quickly as if I could escape the horror that chased me. I didn't dare return to my room. The thought of seeing him again made my skin crawl. So I kept walking, my clothes soaked through from the pouring rain, wandering aimlessly under the cold, endless sky.

I kept walking for a long time, hoping that moving would somehow lighten the heavy weight in my mind. I wandered through the streets without any sense of direction, unaware of where I was going or what I was doing. My heart pounded with fear, and I walked quickly, my steps uneven and unsteady. I didn't dare glance behind me, afraid of what I might see—

> Like a traveler on an empty road,
> Gripped by fear and dread,
> Who, after glancing back once,
> Keeps moving forward, never looking again,
> Because he knows that something awful
> Is lurking just behind him.

I kept walking, hoping that movement would help ease the heavy burden on my mind. I wandered through the streets without thinking about where I was going or what I was doing. My heart pounded with fear, and I moved quickly, my steps uneven, afraid to turn around— terrified of what I might see.

Eventually, I found myself near an inn where coaches and carriages regularly stopped. I wasn't sure why, but I stood there for a few minutes, staring at an approaching coach. As it got closer, I recognized it as the Swiss diligence, and when it finally stopped right in front of me, the door opened. To my surprise, Henry Clerval stepped out.

"My dear Frankenstein!" he exclaimed. "I can't believe how lucky I am to find you here at this very moment!"

Nothing could match the joy I felt upon seeing Clerval. His presence reminded me of my father, Elizabeth, and my home—all the people and places I had been neglecting for so long. I grasped his hand, and for the first time in months, I felt truly happy. The horror and misery that had consumed me suddenly faded, and I welcomed him warmly as we walked toward my college.

Clerval talked excitedly about our mutual friends and how thrilled he was that his father had finally allowed him to come to Ingolstadt. "You wouldn't believe how hard it was to convince my father that education isn't just about bookkeeping," he said with a laugh. "He never believed me, though. He always answered my arguments with the same words as that Dutch schoolmaster from The Vicar of Wakefield: 'I have ten thousand florins a year without Greek. I eat heartily without Greek.' But in the end, his love for me won over his dislike of learning, and he finally let me go on this journey to seek knowledge."

I smiled. "I can't tell you how happy I am to see you. But please, tell me—how are my father, my brothers, and Elizabeth?"

"They're doing well and are very happy, though they do worry about you. They hardly ever hear from you, and I plan to scold you about that myself," Clerval said playfully. But then he suddenly stopped and looked at me more closely. "Victor," he said, his expression shifting to concern, "you look awful! You're pale and thin—have you been sleeping at all?"

I tried to brush off his worries. "You're right," I admitted. "I've been so caught up in my work that I haven't been taking care of myself. But I hope—no, I believe—that it's all over now. I am finally free."

Even as I spoke, I trembled violently. I couldn't bear to think about what had happened the night before, let alone talk about it. I walked faster, eager to reach my college, but as we got closer, a terrible thought struck me—what if the creature was still there? The idea made my skin crawl. I was terrified to see it again, but even more terrified that Henry might see it too.

I quickly asked him to wait at the bottom of the stairs while I went up to check my room. My heart pounded as I reached for the door handle, but suddenly, I hesitated. A cold shiver ran down my spine. Taking a deep breath, I pushed the door open forcefully, the way a child might when expecting a ghost to jump out at them. But there was nothing there.

I stepped inside cautiously. The room was empty. My bedroom, too, was free of the horrible thing I had left behind. I could hardly believe it. Could I be this lucky? Had it really gone? Slowly, as the truth sank in, I felt a rush of relief. Overcome with joy, I clapped my hands and ran back down to Clerval.

We returned to my room together, and a servant brought us breakfast. But I couldn't sit still. It wasn't just happiness—I felt restless, my nerves on edge. My skin tingled, and my heart raced. I couldn't stay in one place. I jumped over chairs, clapped my hands, and even laughed out loud. At first, Clerval thought I was just overjoyed to see him, but as he watched me more closely, he grew concerned. My laughter was too wild, my eyes too bright, and my excitement too unnatural.

"Victor, what's wrong?" he asked, fear creeping into his voice. "Please, stop laughing like that. You don't look well at all. What has happened to you?"

"Don't ask me!" I cried, covering my face with my hands. I thought I saw a shadow—was the monster in the room with us? "He knows! Oh, save me—please, save me!"

My body went rigid with terror, and I collapsed in a fit.

Poor Clerval! What must he have felt in that moment? He had been so excited to see me, only for our happy reunion to turn into something awful. But I wasn't aware of any of it—I was unconscious for a long time.

This was the beginning of a terrible illness that kept me bedridden for months. Through it all, Henry never left my side. He became my only caregiver, looking after me with the deepest kindness and patience. Later, I learned that he had hidden the truth of my condition from my father and Elizabeth. He knew that my father was too old to make such a long journey and that Elizabeth would only suffer if she knew how sick I was. So, instead of worrying them, he took care of me himself, convinced that I would recover.

But I was truly ill, and I know now that without Clerval's constant care, I might not have survived. Even in my fevered state, I could not escape the image of the creature I had brought to life. I spoke about him constantly, raving in my delirium. At first, Henry thought it was just the ramblings of a sick mind, but as I kept returning to the same subject, he began to suspect that something terrible had happened to me.

It took a long time, and I suffered many setbacks, but I slowly began to recover. I remember the first time I truly noticed the world outside again—the trees outside my window had lost their dead leaves, and fresh green buds had started to appear. Spring had arrived, and its warmth and beauty helped heal both my body and my mind. The dark cloud that had hung over me for so long began to lift, and my spirits grew lighter. Before long, I felt almost like my old self again.

"Dearest Clerval," I said one day, "I don't know how to thank you. This entire winter, instead of studying as you planned, you've been stuck taking care of me. How will I ever repay you? I feel terrible for taking up so much of your time."

"You can repay me by focusing on getting better," Clerval said with a smile. "And since you seem to be feeling much better, there's something I'd like to talk to you about—if that's alright?"

I froze. One thing? My stomach twisted with fear. What if he had learned something? What if he was going to bring up the very thing I couldn't even bear to think about?

"Calm down," he said gently, noticing my sudden tension. "If it upsets you, I won't bring it up. But I do think your father and Elizabeth would love to hear from you. They don't know how sick you've been, and they're getting worried because you haven't written."

I let out a deep breath, relieved. "That's all? Of course, my dear friend! How could you think I wouldn't want to write to them? I love them more than anything."

"In that case," Clerval said, smiling, "you'll be glad to know that a letter arrived for you a few days ago. It's from your cousin, I believe."

Chapter 6

Clerval handed me a letter. It was from Elizabeth.

"My Dearest Cousin,

"I have heard that you have been very sick, and even though Henry has written to us often with updates, I still worry about you. You are not allowed to write or even hold a pen, but just one word from you would ease our fears. For weeks, I have expected each letter to be the one that finally contains a message from you, and my pleading has been the only thing keeping my uncle from traveling to Ingolstadt himself. I have stopped him from making such a long and difficult journey, but I have often wished I could make the trip myself. I keep imagining you being cared for by some old nurse who doesn't know your needs and could never look after you with the same love and attention as I would.

"But that is in the past now—Clerval writes that you are recovering. I hope you will confirm this in your own handwriting soon.

"Please get better and come home. You will return to a place full of warmth and happiness, with friends who love you dearly. Your father is still strong and healthy, and the only thing he wants is to see you again and know that you are well. If you were here, you would be so proud of Ernest! He is sixteen now, full of energy and enthusiasm. He wants to follow the Swiss tradition and serve in the military, but my uncle doesn't like the idea of him going to a faraway country. Ernest has never had the patience for study like you did—he sees books as a burden. He would rather be outside, climbing the hills or rowing on the lake. If we don't let him follow his dream, I worry that he may become restless and lose his sense of purpose.

"Not much has changed since you left, except that the younger children have grown. The blue lake and snow-covered mountains are the same as ever, and our home remains peaceful and full of love. My simple daily tasks keep me busy and bring me joy, and my greatest reward is seeing the happy faces of the people around me.

"Since you have been away, only one real change has happened in our household. Do you remember how Justine Moritz came to live with us? You may not, so I will remind you.

"Justine's mother, Madame Moritz, was a widow with four children, and Justine was her third. Her father adored her, but for some strange reason, her mother never showed her kindness. After her father died, her mother treated her even worse. My aunt noticed this and, when Justine was twelve, convinced Madame Moritz to let her come live with us.

"Our country's traditions are different from the monarchies that surround us. Here, people are not divided so strictly by class, and the working class is treated with more respect. A servant in Geneva is not looked down upon the way they are in France or England. When Justine joined our family, she learned to serve, but in our home, being a servant did not mean losing one's dignity or intelligence.

"I remember how much you liked Justine. You once told me that if you were ever in a bad mood, just one look at her happy, open face could lift your spirits. She reminded you of Angelica from Orlando Furioso because she had such a natural charm. My aunt was very fond of her and decided to give her a better education than she had originally planned. Justine was deeply grateful, though she never said so in words. You could see it in her eyes—she adored my aunt and tried to be just like her. She paid close attention to everything my aunt did and even copied her way of speaking and behaving. Even now, she reminds me of her.

"When my aunt passed away, everyone was so overwhelmed with grief that no one thought to comfort Justine, even though she had cared for my aunt with so much love during her illness. The loss affected her deeply, but sadly, more hardships awaited her."

One by one, Justine's brothers and sister passed away, leaving her mother with no children except the daughter she had always neglected. Her mother began to feel guilty, believing that losing her favorite children was a punishment from God for treating Justine unfairly. As a devout Roman Catholic, she turned to her priest, who seemed to confirm her fears. A few months after you left for Ingolstadt, Justine's mother asked her to come back home, hoping to make amends.

The poor girl cried when she had to leave us. Since my aunt's death, she had changed—her grief had softened her, making her gentler and more kind-hearted. Before, she had been lively and full of energy, but sadness had quieted her spirit. Unfortunately, life with her mother did nothing to restore her happiness. The woman could not make up her mind—sometimes, she begged Justine to forgive her for all the cruelty she had shown in the past. But more often, she blamed her for the deaths of her siblings. The constant stress and regret eventually made Madame Moritz ill. At first, her sickness only made her mood worse, but she finally found peace when she passed away at the beginning of winter.

Justine has now returned to us, and I assure you, I love her dearly. She is intelligent, kind, and very beautiful. As I mentioned before, her presence often reminds me of my dear aunt.

I must also tell you a little about our sweet William. Oh, how I wish you could see him! He has grown so tall for his age. His bright blue eyes sparkle with laughter, framed by dark lashes and soft curls. When he smiles, two dimples appear on his rosy cheeks. He is full of joy and already has a few "wives," but his favorite is Louisa Biron, a lovely little girl who is only five years old.

Now, dear Victor, I imagine you'd like to hear some news about the people of Geneva. The beautiful Miss Mansfield has already received visits celebrating her upcoming marriage to an Englishman, John Melbourne, Esq. Her less-attractive sister, Manon, married M. Duvillard, the wealthy banker, last autumn. Your old school friend, Louis Manoir, has had a streak of bad luck since Clerval left Geneva, but he has recovered and is rumored to be engaged to a charming French widow, Madame Tavernier. She is much older than Manoir, but she is well-liked and admired by many.

Writing this letter has lifted my spirits, dear cousin, but as I finish, my worries for you return. Please, Victor, just one word—one line— would be a blessing to us. We are so grateful to Henry for his kindness, for taking care of you, and for keeping us informed.

Take care of yourself, my dear cousin. And I beg you—write!

Elizabeth Lavenza

"Geneva, March 18th, 17—"

"Dear Elizabeth!"

I cried after reading her letter. "I will write back immediately and put their worries to rest." Writing, though, left me exhausted. But my recovery had begun, and I was steadily improving. Two weeks later, I was finally well enough to leave my room.

One of my first tasks after regaining my strength was introducing Clerval to the university professors. This experience, however, was difficult for me. Ever since that terrible night—the end of my experiments and the start of my misery—I had developed a deep hatred for even hearing the name natural philosophy. Though my body had recovered, even the sight of a chemistry tool brought back waves of anxiety. Henry noticed this and removed all my equipment from my sight. He even moved me to a new room, knowing I could no longer bear to be in the one that had served as my laboratory. But all of Henry's efforts to protect me were useless when I had to visit the professors.

M. Waldman was kind, but his praise was unbearable. He spoke warmly about my impressive progress, not realizing how much his words tormented me. I could see he believed my discomfort was due to modesty, so he tried to change the subject, talking instead about the beauty of science itself, hoping to encourage me. What could I do? He meant well, yet every word felt like a fresh wound. It was as if he was carefully setting out the very instruments that would one day be used to torture me. I could barely hide my pain.

Clerval, ever perceptive, quickly changed the conversation, pretending he knew nothing about the subject. I silently thanked him, but I said nothing. He was clearly puzzled by my reaction, but he never once tried to force me to reveal my secret. Even though I loved him like a brother, I could never bring myself to share what haunted me. I feared that speaking about it would only make it more real, more permanent.

M. Krempe, however, was not so considerate. With my nerves already on edge, his blunt and boastful remarks made me feel even worse than M. Waldman's well-intended praise.

"Damn this boy!" he shouted. "M. Clerval, you may not believe it, but this young man has outshined us all! It's true! A few years ago, he thought Cornelius Agrippa's nonsense was as true as the Gospel, and now he's leading the entire university! If he isn't brought down soon, we'll all be embarrassed." He must have noticed the pained look on my face because he quickly added, "Ah, M. Frankenstein is just being modest! Modesty is a fine trait in a young man, wouldn't you say, M. Clerval? I was modest once too—though that stage doesn't last long."

Thankfully, he then launched into a speech about his own achievements, which at least took the attention off me.

Clerval had never shared my love of science, and his interests were completely different from mine. He came to the university to master the languages of the East—Persian, Arabic, and Sanskrit—so that he could build a career filled with adventure. He wanted to do something meaningful with his life, and he saw studying these languages as his path forward. I was easily convinced to join him in these studies. I hated doing nothing, and since I wanted to avoid thinking about the past, I found comfort in working alongside my friend. I wasn't as serious as he was about it—I studied just enough to understand the texts rather than master the languages—but I found great joy in reading them. Their words had a way of lifting my spirits in a way no other literature had before. Their sadness felt comforting, and their joy was deeply moving. Their poetry painted life as a dream of sunshine and gardens, of love and heartbreak. It was so different from the bold, heroic stories of Greece and Rome.

That summer passed quickly as I focused on these new studies, and my return to Geneva was set for late autumn. However, unexpected delays kept me from leaving, and before I knew it, winter had arrived. The roads became too dangerous to travel, forcing me to stay until spring. The delay was frustrating—I longed to see my home and my loved ones—but I had put off my return for so long because I didn't want to leave Clerval alone in an unfamiliar place. Despite my disappointment, the winter months were pleasant, and although spring arrived later than usual, its beauty made up for the long wait.

By May, I was expecting a letter any day to confirm the date of my return. But before I left, Henry suggested we take one last walking tour around the countryside near Ingolstadt to properly say goodbye to the place I had called home for so long. I eagerly agreed. I had always loved long walks, and Clerval had always been my favorite companion on such adventures.

We spent two weeks traveling on foot. My health and happiness, which had already improved, became even stronger as I breathed the fresh air, admired the landscape, and enjoyed my friend's company. I hadn't realized how much my intense studies had isolated me from other people, making me withdrawn. But Henry helped bring me back to life. He reminded me how to appreciate nature again, how to find joy in the simple things. His kindness and warmth pulled me out of the darkness I had been trapped in. I felt like the person I had been years ago—full of love, free of sorrow. When I was truly happy, even the world around me seemed more beautiful. A clear sky, green fields, blooming flowers—these things filled me with pure delight.

Henry was thrilled to see me happy again, and his joy only deepened my own. He did everything he could to amuse me, and I was amazed at his endless creativity. He would make up incredible stories, inspired by the Persian and Arabic literature he loved, or recite my favorite poems. Sometimes, he would challenge me to debates, which he always argued with great passion and skill.

After our journey, we returned to Ingolstadt on a Sunday afternoon. The streets were alive with celebration—peasants danced joyfully, and everywhere we looked, people were laughing and smiling. My own spirits were soaring, and as I walked among them, I felt completely free, full of lightness and joy.

Chapter 7

When I returned, I found a letter from my father:

"My dear Victor,

"You have probably been waiting anxiously for a letter telling you when to come home. At first, I thought of writing just a few short lines to tell you the date, but that would have been too cruel. I cannot keep the truth from you. Imagine expecting a warm and joyful welcome, only to find sorrow and tears instead. My son, how can I bring myself to tell you such terrible news? I know that even now, your eyes are racing over this page, searching for the dreadful words that will confirm your worst fears.

"William is dead.

"Our sweet child, whose laughter filled our home with warmth and happiness, is gone. And Victor—he was murdered.

"I will not try to comfort you just yet; instead, I will tell you exactly what happened.

"Last Thursday, May 7th, Elizabeth, your two brothers, and I went for a walk in Plainpalais. It was a warm, peaceful evening, and we stayed out longer than usual. By the time we decided to head back, the sun had already set. That was when we realized that William and Ernest, who had been walking ahead of us, were nowhere to be found. We waited, hoping they would return soon. After a while, Ernest came back alone, asking if we had seen his brother. He said they had been playing together when William ran off to hide. Ernest searched for him and waited a long time, but William never returned.

"This worried us, and we searched for him until night fell. Elizabeth thought that maybe he had gone home, but when we got back, he wasn't there. I couldn't sleep knowing my little boy was lost in the cold, damp night. So we went back out with torches to continue searching. Elizabeth was beside herself with worry.

"Around five in the morning, I found him. Only the night before, he had been full of life, running and laughing. But now, he lay still and lifeless on the grass, his skin pale and cold. There were dark marks on his neck—proof that someone had strangled him.

"We carried him home, and when Elizabeth saw the look on my face, she immediately knew the terrible truth. She was desperate to see him. At first, I tried to stop her, but she refused to be kept away. When she entered the room where his body lay, she looked at his neck, then suddenly cried out, 'Oh God! I have murdered my darling child!'

"She collapsed, and it was incredibly difficult to bring her back. When she woke, she could do nothing but weep. Between her sobs, she told me that William had begged to wear a locket that held a miniature portrait of your mother. She had finally agreed and given it to him. Now, the locket is missing. We believe it was stolen—and that it was the reason William was killed.

"We have been searching tirelessly for the murderer, but so far, there is no trace of him. And no amount of effort will bring back my beloved son.

"Victor, come home. Only you can comfort Elizabeth. She cannot stop crying and blames herself, even though she did nothing wrong. Her words cut straight to my heart. We are all grieving, but that should be even more reason for you to return to us—to help ease our suffering.

"Your mother, dear Victor—perhaps it is a mercy that she did not live to see her youngest child meet such a cruel and tragic end.

"Come back to us, my son, not with thoughts of hatred or revenge, but with love and kindness. We need healing, not more pain. Step into this house of sorrow with warmth in your heart for those who love you, not with anger toward those who have wronged us.

"Your loving and heartbroken father,

Alphonse Frankenstein."

Since I couldn't enter the city that night, I had to stay in the nearby village of Secheron. It was May 12th, 17—. Sleep would not come, so I decided to visit the place where William had been murdered. Because the gates of Geneva were closed, I had to cross the lake by boat to reach Plainpalais.

As I traveled across the water, I noticed lightning flashing over the peak of Mont Blanc. The storm moved quickly, and when I arrived at my destination, I climbed a small hill to watch its progress. The sky grew darker, and soon, large raindrops began to fall, increasing in intensity with each passing moment.

I left my spot and continued walking, though the wind howled, and the thunder roared overhead. The sound echoed across the mountains—Salêve, Jura, and the distant Alps of Savoy all seemed to repeat the crashing noise. Bright streaks of lightning split the sky, reflecting on the lake like a vast sheet of fire. After each blinding flash, darkness swallowed everything again, leaving me dazed until my eyes adjusted. In Switzerland, storms often appear in different parts of the sky at once, and this night was no exception. The most violent storm raged north of the town, over the part of the lake between Belrive and the village of Copêt. Another storm flickered over Jura, and yet another cast fleeting shadows over the Môle, a mountain to the east of the lake.

As I wandered through the storm, caught between fear and awe, I suddenly saw something move in the darkness. A shadow emerged from behind a group of trees. I froze, staring intently. The next lightning bolt illuminated the figure, revealing its unmistakable form. It was enormous, with a shape more monstrous than any human. My blood ran cold. It was him—the horrible creature I had brought to life.

Why was he here? What reason could he have to lurk in the very place where my brother was murdered? A terrible thought entered my mind, and as soon as I considered it, I knew it must be true. My body trembled violently. I leaned against a tree for support, my teeth chattering.

The figure moved quickly, disappearing into the darkness. A flash of lightning revealed him again, now climbing the nearly vertical side of Mont Salêve, the mountain that bordered Plainpalais. Within moments, he reached the top and vanished.

I stood frozen in place, overwhelmed. The storm had begun to fade, but the rain continued to pour. The entire landscape was shrouded in darkness. My mind raced as I recalled the events I had tried so hard to forget—the long months of my experiments, the dreadful night I gave life to the creature, and his escape. Nearly two years had passed since that fateful night. Could this have been his first crime?

I had released a monster into the world, a being that found joy in violence and suffering. Had he taken my brother's life?

I spent the rest of the night outside, cold and soaked to the bone, but I hardly noticed. My imagination was filled with horror. I had created this creature. I had given him strength, intelligence, and the ability to move among mankind. But in doing so, I had unleashed a nightmare—one that seemed determined to destroy everything I loved. In that moment, I saw him as my own dark reflection, a creature born of my ambition, now set loose to bring ruin upon me.

I got up from where I was sitting and continued walking, even though the storm grew stronger with every passing moment. Thunder crashed loudly above me, echoing across the mountains—Salêve, Jura, and the distant Alps of Savoy. Bright flashes of lightning lit up the sky, making the lake below look like a vast, burning surface. But as soon as the lightning faded, everything was swallowed by complete darkness again, leaving my eyes struggling to adjust. The storm, as was common in Switzerland, raged in several areas at once. The fiercest part was directly north of town, over the section of the lake between the Belrive promontory and the village of Copêt. Another storm flickered dimly over Jura, while yet another cast shadows over the Môle, a mountain to the east of the lake.

As I watched the powerful and terrifying storm, I kept moving, my pace quickening. The wild energy in the sky lifted my spirits, and I suddenly raised my hands and cried out, "William, dear angel! This is your funeral, this is your song of mourning!" The moment those words left my lips, I saw something shift in the darkness. A figure emerged from behind a group of trees. I stood still, staring intently, trying to make out its shape. Then, another bolt of lightning flashed, revealing the horrifying truth—I could see the enormous size of the figure, its inhuman form more grotesque than any ordinary person could ever be.

It was him—the wretched creature I had brought to life.

What was he doing here? A chilling thought entered my mind. Could he have been the one who murdered my brother? The idea made me shudder, but the moment it crossed my mind, I knew it had to be true. My body trembled violently, and I had to lean against a tree to keep from collapsing.

The figure moved quickly, vanishing into the darkness. No human could have done what had been done to William. He was the murderer! I had no doubt. The mere thought of it was proof enough. I wanted to chase after the creature, to hunt him down—but it would have been pointless. Another flash of lightning revealed him again, this time climbing the sheer, rocky side of Mont Salêve, a steep mountain bordering Plainpalais. Within moments, he reached the top and disappeared.

I stood there, frozen. The thunder had stopped, but the rain still poured, and the night remained dark and heavy. My mind raced with thoughts I had tried so hard to forget—the endless nights of my experiments, the moment my creation had first opened its lifeless eyes, and its terrifying escape. It had been nearly two years since that awful night. Had this been his first act of violence?

I had let a monster loose upon the world, a creature that seemed to take pleasure in destruction and suffering. And now, he had murdered my brother.

I spent the rest of the night outside, cold and drenched, but I barely noticed the discomfort. My mind was trapped in a whirlwind of horror and regret. I had created this being, given him strength and a will of his own, only for him to use that power to bring terror and death. It felt as if he were a part of me—an extension of my own soul, an evil shadow I had unleashed, now bent on destroying everything I loved.

At last, the sun began to rise, and I made my way toward the town. The gates were open, and I hurried to my father's house. My first thought was to tell them what I knew—to reveal the truth about the murderer and have them chase him down immediately. But then I hesitated. What could I possibly say? That I had built a living being with my own hands and that he had now become a killer? That I had seen him lurking in the darkness near the scene of the crime?

I remembered the terrible fever I had suffered right after creating him. People would think I had lost my mind. If I had heard such a story from someone else, I wouldn't have believed them either. And even if they did believe me, how could anyone possibly catch him? He had the strength and speed to climb sheer cliffs—no ordinary person could hope to stop him.

So, I decided to keep silent.

It was around five in the morning when I arrived home. I told the servants not to wake the family and went into the library to wait for them.

As I stood there, I realized it had been six years since I had last been in this room, just before leaving for Ingolstadt. It felt like a different lifetime. I looked up at a painting of my mother above the fireplace. It showed her kneeling in despair beside her father's coffin. Her expression was sorrowful, yet she still carried an air of dignity and beauty. Below that painting was a small portrait of William. Tears filled my eyes as I gazed at it.

While I was lost in thought, my younger brother Ernest entered the room. He had heard me arrive and rushed to greet me.

"Welcome home, my dear Victor," he said. "Oh, how I wish you had come back three months ago! Everything was happy then. But now, you return to nothing but sadness. I hope your presence will help our father, though—he's barely holding on after what happened. And maybe you can convince poor Elizabeth to stop blaming herself. Poor William! He was our joy, our pride!"

Tears streamed down Ernest's face. A deep, unbearable grief settled over me. Before this moment, I had only imagined the pain of losing William. But now, standing in my childhood home, hearing my brother's words, the weight of reality hit me like a crushing blow.

I tried to comfort Ernest and asked about our father and Elizabeth.

"She needs comfort more than anyone," Ernest replied sadly. "She blames herself for William's death, and it's breaking her heart. But now that they've caught the murderer—"

I froze. "The murderer has been caught?!" I gasped. "That's impossible! No one could have chased him down! No human could have stopped him! I saw him last night—he was free!"

"I don't understand what you mean," my brother said, clearly confused. "But this discovery has only made things worse for us. At first, no one believed it. Even now, Elizabeth refuses to accept it, despite all the evidence. And honestly, who could imagine that Justine Moritz, who was always so kind and loving toward our family, could be guilty of such a terrible crime?"

"Justine Moritz? No! Poor girl, she can't be the one accused! That must be a mistake—everyone must know that! No one actually believes it, do they, Ernest?"

"At first, no one did," he admitted. "But some things have come to light that make it hard to doubt. And the way she's been acting—so nervous and confused—has only made her look more guilty. I hate to say it, but I don't see how she can prove her innocence. Her trial is today, and you'll hear everything then."

Ernest then explained that on the morning William's body was found, Justine had become ill and was in bed for several days. While she was sick, one of the servants went through the clothes she had worn the night of the murder and found the locket with our mother's picture inside her pocket—the very same locket William had been carrying when he disappeared. Thinking this was proof of her guilt, the servant showed it to another, and without telling the family, they took it straight to the authorities. Justine was arrested immediately. When confronted, her nervous and confused behavior made her look even more suspicious.

It was a shocking story, but I didn't believe a word of it. I answered firmly, "You're all wrong. I know who the real murderer is. Justine, poor Justine, is innocent."

At that moment, my father entered the room. His face showed deep sorrow, but he tried to greet me warmly. After our sad exchange, he attempted to talk about something other than our tragedy, but Ernest interrupted.

"Father! Victor says he knows who killed William!"

"We already know, unfortunately," my father replied, shaking his head. "And I wish we had never discovered such awful betrayal from someone we trusted."

"Father, you're wrong. Justine didn't do it!" I insisted.

"If she is truly innocent, then may God prevent her from being punished as if she were guilty," he said. "Her trial is today. I hope with all my heart that she will be cleared."

His words gave me some comfort. I was completely sure that Justine—or any human—could not have committed this crime. No evidence should be strong enough to convict her. But I also knew I could never reveal the truth. No one would believe my story; they would think I had lost my mind. Who, other than me, could possibly accept the existence of the monster I had created with my own hands?

A few moments later, Elizabeth joined us. Time had changed her since I last saw her. She had grown even more beautiful, with the same energy and honesty, but now mixed with deeper emotion and wisdom. She greeted me with warmth.

"Victor, your arrival gives me hope," she said. "Maybe you can find a way to prove Justine's innocence. If she is convicted, who can ever feel safe? I believe in her as much as I believe in myself. This whole situation is unbearable—we haven't just lost sweet William, but now we may also lose Justine to an even worse fate. If she is found guilty, I will never be happy again. But I can't believe that will happen. She has to be proven innocent, and then—despite everything—I can try to feel joy again."

"She is innocent, Elizabeth," I assured her. "And that will be proven. Don't worry. Trust that she will be cleared."

"You're so kind and good!" she said, her voice shaking. "Everyone else believes she's guilty, and it has made me feel so hopeless. I know she couldn't have done this, but seeing others turn against her has been unbearable." Tears welled in her eyes.

"My dear niece," my father said gently, "wipe away your tears. If she truly is innocent, trust in our laws to see the truth. I will do everything in my power to make sure the trial is fair."

Chapter 8

We spent several sorrowful hours waiting for eleven o'clock, when the trial was set to begin. My father and the rest of my family were required to attend as witnesses, so I went with them to the courthouse. Throughout the entire trial, I suffered unbearable torment. It was unbearable to think that my actions—my reckless curiosity—could lead to the deaths of two innocent people: one, a happy, innocent child; the other, a young woman whose life would be taken in a way that would make her death even more terrible. Justine was kind and good, and she had once had a promising future. Now, she was about to be sent to a disgraceful death, and it was all because of me. A thousand times, I wished I could take the blame for the crime, but I had not even been there when it happened. If I confessed, I would only seem insane, and it would do nothing to save Justine.

Justine appeared calm as she entered the courtroom. She was dressed in mourning, and though her face had always been lovely, the seriousness of her situation gave her an even more delicate beauty. She looked innocent and did not seem to be afraid, even as the crowd stared at her with hatred. Any kindness her beauty might have inspired in them was completely erased by the terrible crime she was accused of. She forced herself to stay composed, knowing that her earlier confusion had been used as evidence against her. When she entered the courtroom, her eyes searched for us, and when she found us, a single tear welled up. But she quickly wiped it away and looked at us with sorrow and love, a silent testament to her innocence.

The trial began. The prosecutor laid out the charges, and then several witnesses were called to testify. The evidence against Justine was shocking, and anyone who didn't know the truth, as I did, might have believed it. She had been out all night on the night of the murder, and a market-woman had seen her near the place where William's body was later found. When the woman asked what she was doing, Justine had acted strangely and given a confused, meaningless answer. She returned home at around eight in the morning, and when asked where she had been, she said she had been searching for William and begged to know if he had been found. When they showed her his body, she collapsed in hysterics and was bedridden for days. Then came the most damning piece of evidence—the missing locket with my mother's picture. A servant had found it in Justine's pocket. When Elizabeth, barely able to speak, confirmed that she had placed it around William's neck just before he went missing, the entire courtroom erupted in shock and outrage.

Then, Justine was asked to speak in her own defense. As the trial had gone on, her expression had changed. First, she had looked surprised. Then horrified. Then deeply miserable. She struggled to hold back tears, but when she was told to speak, she pulled herself together and addressed the court in a steady but trembling voice.

"God knows that I am innocent," she said. "But I know that simply saying so will not clear me. I can only explain the truth about the events that seem to be against me, and I hope that my character, which has always been good, will lead my judges to see me as innocent if anything about this case remains unclear."

She then explained that Elizabeth had given her permission to spend the evening at her aunt's house in Chêne, a village about a league from Geneva. She returned around nine o'clock, where she met a man who asked if she had seen anything about the missing child. Alarmed by this, she spent several hours searching for him. But by the time she reached the city gates, they had been closed for the night, so she was forced to take shelter in a barn on a farm. She didn't want to wake the owners, though they knew her well. Most of the night, she stayed awake, but she believed she had dozed off for a little while before being startled awake by footsteps. At dawn, she left the barn and went out again to search for William. If she had passed near the place where his body was found, it was purely by accident. And as for the market-woman's claims that she had been confused—it made sense. She had spent a sleepless night searching for a lost child, and at that point, she still didn't know what had happened to him. As for the locket, she had no idea how it ended up in her pocket.

"I know," she continued, "that this single piece of evidence weighs heavily against me, but I have no way to explain it. I can only guess how it might have happened. But I have never had an enemy in my life, and I cannot imagine that anyone would deliberately set me up to be condemned for such a crime. Could the real murderer have placed it in my pocket? I don't see how. And if they did, why would they have stolen the locket, only to get rid of it so soon?"

She looked around the courtroom with deep sadness.

"I leave my fate in the hands of my judges, though I see no hope for myself. I only ask that a few witnesses be called to testify to my character. If their words are not enough to outweigh the case against me, then I will be condemned—though I swear on my soul that I am innocent."

Several witnesses were brought forward to speak on Justine's behalf—people who had known her for years and could confirm her good character. However, many were too afraid to defend her, fearing what others might think if they stood up for someone accused of such a terrible crime. Elizabeth realized that even this final chance—

Justine's history of kindness and good behavior—was failing to protect her. Despite her overwhelming emotions, she gathered her courage and asked for permission to address the court.

"I am the cousin of the murdered child," she said, "or rather his sister, since I was raised by his parents and lived with them long before he was born. It may seem inappropriate for me to speak here, but when I see an innocent person about to be condemned because her so-called friends are too afraid to defend her, I must speak. I know Justine well. I lived in the same house as her—once for five years, and again for nearly two. During that time, I saw nothing but kindness and goodness in her. She cared for Madame Frankenstein, my aunt, with love and dedication during her final illness. Later, she nursed her own mother through a long sickness, earning the admiration of everyone who knew her. After that, she returned to my uncle's home, where she was loved by all. She adored William and cared for him like a mother. I have no doubt that she is innocent, despite the so-called evidence against her. She had no reason to harm him. And as for the necklace that has been used as proof of her guilt—if she had truly wanted it, I would have gladly given it to her, because I trust and value her so much."

A murmur spread through the courtroom after Elizabeth's passionate words, but it was not in Justine's favor. The people admired Elizabeth's loyalty, but their anger toward Justine only grew. They now saw her as not just a murderer, but also an ungrateful betrayer. Justine, overwhelmed, could only weep silently.

I was tormented throughout the trial. I knew Justine was innocent. There was no doubt in my mind. But was it possible that the same monster who had murdered my brother had also set her up to take the blame? The horror of the thought was unbearable. When I realized that both the public and the judges had already made up their minds against her, I could take no more. I ran from the courtroom in agony. The pain Justine felt could not compare to mine—her innocence gave her strength, while guilt and remorse tore me apart.

That night was one of pure misery. The next morning, I returned to the courthouse, but my throat was dry, and I could barely bring myself to ask what had happened. The officer, seeing my distress, guessed why I had come and told me the verdict—Justine had been found guilty.

I cannot describe the despair that consumed me in that moment. I had thought I had known horror before, but this was something worse. My heart felt as if it were breaking. The officer added that Justine had already confessed to the crime.

"Of course," he said, "the evidence was strong enough without a confession, but it's always better when the guilty admit their crimes. Our judges don't like convicting someone based on indirect proof alone."

I was stunned. Had I been wrong? Had I imagined everything? Could I really be as mad as the world would think if I revealed what I knew? Confused and shaken, I hurried home, where Elizabeth was waiting anxiously for news.

"My cousin," I told her, "the verdict is what you expected. The judges would rather condemn ten innocent people than let one guilty person go free. But Justine has confessed."

This news was a terrible shock to Elizabeth. She had firmly believed in Justine's innocence.

"How can I ever trust anyone again?" she whispered. "I loved her like a sister. How could she deceive us with such an innocent face? I thought I knew her heart, yet she has committed murder."

Not long after, we received word that Justine wanted to see Elizabeth. My father advised against it but left the choice to her.

"Yes," Elizabeth said. "I will go, even if she is guilty. Victor, you must come with me. I cannot do this alone."

The idea of visiting Justine in prison filled me with dread, but I could not refuse.

We entered the dark, gloomy cell and saw Justine sitting on a pile of straw, her hands chained, her head resting on her knees. When she saw us, she immediately stood and, as soon as we were left alone with her, she collapsed at Elizabeth's feet, sobbing. Elizabeth knelt beside her, weeping too.

"Oh, Justine!" Elizabeth cried. "Why did you take away my last bit of hope? I believed in you, and even though I was so sad, I was not as miserable as I am now."

Justine looked up, her face streaked with tears. "Do you really think I am such a terrible person? Have you also turned against me, believing I am a murderer?" Her voice broke with sobs.

Elizabeth gently lifted her. "Get up, Justine. Why do you kneel if you are innocent? I am not your enemy. I believed in you despite all the evidence, but then I heard you confessed. If that was a lie, then tell me now, and I will never doubt you again."

Justine took a deep breath. "I did confess," she said quietly, "but it was a lie. I only said it to get forgiveness for my sins. But now that false confession weighs heavier on my heart than anything else. May God forgive me. Ever since I was found guilty, the priest has pressured me over and over. He threatened me, told me I was a monster, and warned that I would go to hell if I refused to confess. I had no one to support me. Everyone looked at me as if I was doomed, as if I was already damned. What else could I do? In a moment of weakness, I said what they wanted to hear. But now I know—I have never felt more truly miserable than I do at this moment."

She paused, crying, then continued, "It breaks my heart, dear lady, to think that you might believe I could commit such a terrible crime. Your kind aunt trusted me, and you always treated me with love. How could I do something so evil? Sweet William, my precious child! Soon I will see you again in heaven, where we will all be happy. That thought gives me comfort as I face my shameful death."

"Oh, Justine! Forgive me for even doubting you for a moment. But why did you confess? Don't lose hope, my dear friend. I will do everything I can to prove your innocence. I will plead, I will beg, I will make your accusers see the truth. You won't die! I won't allow it. You, my childhood companion, my dear friend, my sister—how could I bear to lose you this way?"

Justine shook her head sadly. "I'm not afraid to die," she said. "That fear is behind me. God has given me strength, and I will face whatever comes. This world has only brought me pain, and if you remember me as someone who was wrongly accused, I will accept my fate. Please, my dear lady, learn from me—accept what life brings with patience and faith."

As they spoke, I stood silently in the corner of the prison cell, trying to hide the overwhelming guilt that consumed me. Despair? How could anyone else speak of despair? Justine, who would soon face death, did not suffer as I did. The pain I felt was unbearable. My whole body trembled, and I let out a deep, anguished groan. Justine looked up in alarm. When she saw me, she came closer and said, "Dear sir, you are very kind to visit me. Surely, you don't believe I am guilty?"

I couldn't answer. "No, Justine," Elizabeth said. "Victor believes in your innocence even more than I do. Even when he heard that you had confessed, he didn't believe it."

Justine gave a faint smile. "I am so grateful. In these final moments, knowing that people still care about me brings me peace. Your kindness makes my suffering easier to bear. Now that I know you and your cousin believe in me, I feel as though I can face what's coming."

Even as she tried to comfort us, she was the one who needed comfort most. She had found acceptance, but I—who was truly to blame—felt nothing but torment. Elizabeth cried as well, but her sorrow was pure, the sadness of someone innocent. My suffering, however, was like a fire burning inside me, and nothing could put it out. We stayed with Justine for several hours, and it was only with great difficulty that Elizabeth was able to leave. "I wish I could die with you," she sobbed. "I don't want to live in such a cruel world."

Justine forced a small smile, though tears filled her eyes. She hugged Elizabeth tightly and whispered, "Goodbye, dear lady. Sweet Elizabeth, my only true friend. May heaven bless you and keep you safe. I hope this is the last sorrow you ever have to bear. Live, be happy, and spread that happiness to others."

The next morning, Justine was executed. Elizabeth's heartfelt plea to the judges failed to change their minds. My own desperate attempts to convince them were useless. When I saw their cold expressions and heard their heartless reasoning, my own confession froze on my lips. I might as well have admitted I was insane—it wouldn't have saved her. And so, Justine was sentenced to die for a crime she did not commit.

The guilt inside me was unbearable, but when I looked at Elizabeth's silent grief, I felt an even greater pain. This was my fault! My father's sorrow, the emptiness in our once-happy home—it was all because of me! You cry now, my beloved family, but these are not the last tears you will shed. More suffering will come, more losses will follow. And I, Frankenstein—the son, the brother, the friend who would have given his life for you—have instead brought only misery. If only death could put an end to this destruction, but I knew the worst was yet to come.

I saw it all in my mind as I stood by the graves of William and Justine—the first, but not the last, victims of my terrible mistake.

Chapter 9

Nothing feels worse than the silence that follows after intense emotions. When things happen quickly, filling the heart with hope or fear, the sudden stillness afterward feels empty and unbearable. Justine was gone. She had found peace. But I was still here, trapped in my own misery, weighed down by guilt that I could never escape. Sleep refused to come. I wandered without purpose, like a lost soul, haunted by the terrible things I had done.

Yet, I had once been kind, full of good intentions. I had started my life wanting to help others, believing I could make a difference. But that dream had been shattered. Instead of the comfort of knowing I had done something good, I was left with nothing but regret. My heart was caught in a never-ending torment, one too deep for words to ever describe.

This overwhelming misery began to affect my health, which had never fully recovered from my first shock. I avoided people. The sound of laughter or happiness felt like torture. My only comfort was solitude—deep, silent, and endless.

My father noticed the change in me and tried to help. He spoke with the wisdom of a man whose heart was at peace, hoping to give me strength. "Victor," he said, "do you think I don't suffer? No one could love a child more than I loved your brother." His voice broke, and tears filled his eyes. "But we must not drown in our grief. We owe it to those who are still here to move forward, to not let our sorrow destroy us. If we let sadness take over, we become useless, unable to live or help those who need us."

His words were wise, but they didn't apply to me. If my grief had been pure sorrow, I would have hidden it and tried to comfort my family. But guilt and fear poisoned my pain, making it impossible to bear. I could only look at my father with hopeless eyes and try to avoid him.

Around this time, we moved to our house in Belrive, which was a relief for me. The strict rules in Geneva—such as the city gates closing at night—had made me feel trapped. In Belrive, I felt free. After my family went to sleep, I would take a boat onto the lake, spending hours alone on the water. Sometimes, I let the wind carry me wherever it wanted. Other times, I rowed out into the middle of the lake and let the boat drift while I was lost in my own miserable thoughts.

There were moments when everything around me was peaceful— the lake was calm, the night was quiet, and I was the only restless thing disturbing the beauty of the scene. Except for the occasional bat or the croaking of frogs near the shore, the world was silent. And in those moments, I was tempted to throw myself into the lake, to let the water close over me and end my suffering forever. But then I thought of Elizabeth, my brave and loving Elizabeth, who depended on me. I thought of my father and my surviving brother—could I abandon them and leave them helpless against the monster I had created?

These thoughts made me break down in tears. I wished I could find peace so that I could bring them comfort, but I knew that was impossible. My guilt destroyed any hope I had. I had unleashed an evil that could never be undone, and I feared that the monster would strike again. I had a terrible feeling that the worst was yet to come, that he would commit a crime so horrifying that it would make everything before seem small in comparison. As long as I still had people I loved, I knew I could never stop being afraid.

My hatred for the creature was beyond words. The thought of him filled me with rage. My eyes burned, my body shook, and all I wanted was to destroy him. I wished I could chase him to the ends of the earth, to the tallest mountain, just to push him off and rid the world of him forever. I longed to see him again—not out of fear, but so that I could unleash all my fury upon him and make him pay for the deaths of William and Justine.

Our home was filled with grief. My father's health suffered under the weight of his sorrow. Elizabeth had become quiet and withdrawn. She no longer found joy in the things that used to make her happy. To her, any pleasure felt like an insult to the dead. She believed that eternal mourning was the only way to honor the loved ones she had lost. The girl who once walked beside me, dreaming of the future, was now weighed down by sadness.

One evening, she spoke to me with a heavy heart. "Victor, ever since Justine's terrible death, I see the world differently. Before, when I heard stories of crime or injustice, they felt distant—things that happened in books or to people far away. But now, I know that misery is real, and people can be cruel. And yet… I know I'm being unfair. Everyone truly believed Justine was guilty. If she had done what they accused her of—if she had killed a child she loved just for a few jewels—then she would have been the most evil person imaginable. If that had been the case, I might have agreed she didn't deserve to live among us. But she was innocent. I know it. You know it. And that only makes it worse.

"When lies can look so much like the truth, how can anyone ever feel safe? I feel like I'm walking on the edge of a cliff, surrounded by people who want to push me over. William and Justine were murdered, and the real killer is still out there, free, maybe even respected. But even if I were to be sentenced to death for a crime I didn't commit, I would rather suffer than be like him."

I listened to these words in complete agony. I wasn't the murderer in action, but in reality, I was responsible. Elizabeth saw the pain on my face and gently took my hand.

"My dear friend, you have to calm yourself," she said. "This tragedy has affected me deeply—God knows how much—but you seem to suffer even more. There is a look of despair in your eyes, sometimes even anger, that frightens me. Victor, let go of these dark feelings. Think of the people who love you, who rely on you for happiness. Have we lost the ability to bring you joy? As long as we have each other, as long as we stay true to our love, we can still find peace here, in this beautiful land. What could possibly take that away from us?"

But even her comforting words, spoken with so much love, could not chase away the darkness inside me. As she spoke, I moved closer to her, as if fearing that at any moment, the monster would come and take her away too.

Neither love nor friendship, nor the beauty of nature, could free me from my suffering. It was like I was trapped in a thick, unbreakable cloud of misery. I felt like a wounded deer, dragging itself away to a quiet place to die, staring at the arrow that had pierced it—just as I was trapped, tormented by my own actions.

At times, I could fight against my despair. But other times, the storm of emotions inside me became unbearable, and I had to escape—to run, to move, to distract myself in any way possible. In one of these desperate moments, I suddenly left home, heading toward the Alpine valleys, hoping that the power and vastness of nature would help me forget my pain. My steps led me toward the valley of Chamounix, a place I had often visited as a child. Six years had passed since then. I was completely changed, but those ancient, unshaken mountains remained the same.

I traveled the first part of my journey on horseback. Later, I rented a mule, which was more suited to the rough mountain roads. The weather was pleasant. It was the middle of August, nearly two months after Justine's death—the moment I marked as the beginning of all my suffering. As I ventured deeper into the Arve Valley, I felt a slight relief from the weight on my soul. Towering mountains surrounded me, and steep cliffs loomed overhead. The sound of the river crashing against the rocks and the waterfalls roaring in the distance reminded me of a power greater than anything I had ever known. I no longer felt fear or submission toward anything less powerful than the force that had created and controlled these elements.

The higher I climbed, the more breathtaking the scenery became. Ruined castles clung to the cliffs of pine-covered mountains. The wild Arve River rushed through the valley, while cottages peeked out from between the trees. It was a stunning sight. But what made it truly magnificent were the mighty Alps, their shining white peaks stretching toward the sky like they belonged to another world, home to a different kind of being.

I crossed the bridge of Pélissier, where the river had carved a deep ravine. As I climbed the mountain beside it, I finally entered the valley of Chamounix. This valley was grand and awe-inspiring, but not as green and picturesque as Servox, which I had just passed through. Here, the towering mountains of ice and snow formed the valley's walls. No more castles or fertile fields were in sight. Massive glaciers reached down to the road, and I could hear the distant rumble of avalanches as they crashed down the mountainside. In the distance, Mont Blanc—

magnificent, towering above all else—stood with its white, snowy peak rising above the surrounding mountains.

For the first time in what felt like forever, I felt brief moments of happiness. A bend in the road, a familiar sight from my childhood, or a sudden memory would transport me back to simpler times. The wind whispered through the trees, and for a moment, nature herself seemed to comfort me, telling me to let go of my sorrow.

But this peace never lasted. The moment of relief would pass, and once again, I would be trapped in my grief. I would urge my mule forward, trying to escape my thoughts, my fears, and—most of all— myself. At times, overwhelmed by despair, I would jump off and collapse on the grass, unable to bear the weight of my suffering.

At last, I arrived at the village of Chamounix. My body and mind were utterly exhausted. For a while, I sat by the window, watching pale flashes of lightning flicker above Mont Blanc, listening to the river Arve roar below. The steady sound of rushing water seemed to soothe me, dulling my overwhelming emotions. As I laid my head on the pillow, I felt sleep creeping in. I welcomed its arrival, thankful for the temporary escape it would bring.

Chapter 10

The next day, I wandered through the valley, exploring its vast and breathtaking landscape. I stood beside the icy waters of the Arveiron River, which flowed from a massive glacier. This glacier, slowly moving down from the mountaintop, seemed to block the valley with its frozen wall. Towering mountains surrounded me, their rugged cliffs rising high above. The air was still, broken only by the sound of rushing water or the occasional thunderous crash of falling ice and avalanches. Sometimes, I could hear the deep cracking of the glacier as it shifted under invisible forces, as if it were a mere plaything in the hands of nature.

In the face of such powerful beauty, I found the only comfort I was capable of feeling. These immense landscapes lifted my spirit, making my own suffering feel small in comparison. Though they did not take away my grief, they helped to calm it. They distracted my mind, pulling it away—at least for a little while—from the dark thoughts that had consumed me for so long. That night, as I drifted to sleep, my dreams were filled with images of the grand scenery I had admired. Snow-covered peaks, shimmering mountaintops, endless forests of pine, deep rocky valleys, and mighty eagles soaring through the clouds—all surrounded me in my dreams, bringing a rare sense of peace.

But when I woke the next morning, all those uplifting feelings had vanished. My heart was heavy again, filled with the same sorrow as before. The sky was gray, and rain poured down in endless streams. Thick mist covered the mountaintops, hiding the familiar sights that had comforted me the day before. Still, I refused to let the storm stop me. I wanted to seek out those mighty mountains, even if I had to travel through fog and rain to find them. What did the weather matter to me? My mind was already trapped in a storm of its own.

I had my mule brought to the door and decided to climb to the top of Montanvert. I remembered the feeling I had the first time I saw its massive glacier, an awe so powerful that it lifted my spirit beyond my troubles. Seeing such wild, untamed beauty always had a way of making my worries seem small, helping me escape the weight of daily life. I chose to go alone, without a guide, because I knew the path well, and I did not want anything to disturb the solitude of the journey.

The climb was steep, with the trail zigzagging back and forth to help travelers navigate the nearly vertical mountainside. The landscape was harsh and desolate. Everywhere, there were signs of past avalanches—fallen trees lay shattered on the ground, some completely destroyed, others leaning against rocks or tangled with other trees. As I climbed higher, the trail cut across patches of snow, with loose stones rolling down from above. One section was particularly dangerous— any loud noise, even a raised voice, could send an avalanche crashing down. The pine trees were short and dark, adding to the serious, almost somber feeling of the place.

I looked down at the valley below. Thick mist rose from the rivers, swirling into heavy clouds that wrapped around the mountains in the distance. Their peaks disappeared into the fog, blending into the dark sky, while the rain continued to fall. The whole scene filled me with a deep sadness.

I wondered—why do people take pride in having emotions that set them apart from animals? Our feelings don't bring us freedom; they only make life harder. If we only cared about basic needs like hunger and thirst, we might be at peace. But instead, we are shaken by every little thing—a word, a memory, or even a simple scene—tossed about like leaves in the wind.

We sleep, but even dreams can bring pain.
We wake, but a single troubling thought can ruin the day.
Whether we feel, think, or try to reason—whether we laugh or cry,
Hold onto sadness or push our worries aside—
It makes no difference, because happiness and sorrow
Can both vanish just as easily as they came.
What was true yesterday may not be true tomorrow,
For nothing lasts forever except change itself.

By the time I reached the top of the climb, it was nearly noon. I sat on a rock overlooking the vast stretch of ice below me. A thick mist covered everything, hiding both the glacier and the surrounding mountains. Then, a strong breeze swept the fog away, and I made my way down onto the ice. The surface was uneven, like a frozen ocean caught in a storm, with deep cracks and ridges rising and falling unpredictably. The glacier stretched nearly a league wide, but it took me almost two hours to cross. On the other side, a towering rock wall stood in front of me. From where I was, I could see Montanvert across the distance, with the mighty Mont Blanc rising above it, standing in all its breathtaking majesty. I stood in a sheltered spot among the rocks, gazing at the incredible scene before me. The vast river of ice wound between towering mountains, their snow-covered peaks shining above the clouds. For a brief moment, my sadness lifted, replaced by a strange sense of peace. I whispered, "If spirits truly wander and do not rest in their graves, let me have this moment of peace—or take me with you, away from this world."

As I spoke, I suddenly noticed a figure in the distance, moving toward me at an unnatural speed. It leapt effortlessly over the deep cracks in the ice—places where I had stepped carefully to avoid falling. As it came closer, I realized with horror that it was the monster I had created. His towering figure and unnatural appearance sent a shiver through me. A wave of dizziness came over me, and my vision blurred, but the cold mountain air quickly revived me. I steadied myself and prepared to fight. Every part of me burned with rage and hatred as I waited for him to approach. His face, twisted with pain, anger, and cruelty, was almost too horrible to look at, but I hardly noticed—I was consumed by fury. At first, I was too angry to even speak, but then I found my voice and shouted words full of disgust and loathing.

"You vile creature!" I screamed. "How dare you come near me? Do you not fear my wrath? You should tremble at the thought of what I will do to you! Get away from me, worthless monster! Or no—stay! Stay so that I can crush you beneath my foot! Oh, if only I could wipe you from existence and bring back those you have so cruelly murdered!"

The creature remained calm and replied, "I knew you would react this way. All men hate the miserable. And who could be more wretched than I? Even you, my own creator, despise and reject me. Yet we are connected, bound together in a way that only death can break. You plan to kill me, as if my life means nothing. But listen to me—I will leave you and the rest of humanity in peace if you do your duty to me. If you refuse, I will bring destruction, and death will feast on the blood of those you love."

"Evil monster!" I shouted. "Even hell would not be enough punishment for what you have done! You blame me for your creation? Then come closer so I can end the life I foolishly gave you!"

Blinded by rage, I lunged at him, determined to destroy him with my own hands.

But he easily dodged my attack and said, "Calm yourself! Hear me out before you act in anger. Have I not suffered enough? Must you add to my misery? No matter how painful my existence is, I still cling to life, and I will fight to survive. Remember, you made me stronger than you. I am taller, my limbs are more flexible, and I could easily overpower you. But I will not fight you. I am your creation, and I will obey you—if you fulfill the duty you owe me. Frankenstein, you treat everyone else fairly, yet you refuse me even the smallest kindness. You, of all people, owe me justice, even mercy. I should have been your Adam, but instead, you have cast me away like the devil himself, banishing me from happiness without reason. I see joy all around me, yet I am forever locked out. I was once kind and good, but misery has turned me into what you see now. Give me a reason to be happy, and I will be good once more."

"Get away from me!" I shouted. "I will not listen! There is nothing between us but hatred. Leave now, or fight me, and one of us will not survive."

"How can I make you listen to me? Will you not show even a little kindness to the creature who begs for your compassion? Believe me, Frankenstein, I was once good and full of love for others. But now, am I not completely alone? Even you, my own creator, hate me—how can I expect anything better from the rest of mankind, who owe me nothing? Everywhere I go, they reject me. I have no home except these cold, empty mountains and glaciers. I have wandered here for days, and only these icy caves offer me shelter because they are the only places humans do not claim. I welcome the bleak sky above me because even it is kinder than people. If mankind knew I existed, they would all try to destroy me, just like you do. So why should I not hate them as they hate me? I will not make peace with my enemies. I am miserable, and I will make them share in my suffering.

But you have the power to change this. You can prevent the disaster that will otherwise consume not just you and your family, but thousands of others. Show me mercy instead of disgust. Listen to my story. When you have heard everything, then judge me—whether to pity me or cast me aside. But at least hear me out. Even criminals are given a chance to defend themselves before they are punished. Listen to me, Frankenstein. You call me a murderer, yet you would kill your own creation without hesitation. What justice is that? But I am not asking for mercy—I only ask you to hear my story. Then, if you still want to destroy me, do as you will."

"Why do you make me remember," I responded angrily, "the terrible truth that I am the one who brought you into this world? I cannot stand the thought! Cursed be the day, you vile monster, that you first saw the light! Cursed be the hands that created you, though they are my own! You have made my life unbearable. I cannot even think about whether I am being fair to you or not. Just go! Get out of my sight!"

The creature raised his hands in front of my face and said, "Then let me give you what you want, my creator." I pushed them away violently, but he continued, "You may shut your eyes, but you can still hear me. You can still choose to show me kindness. By the goodness that I once had, I ask this of you. Listen to my story—it is long and strange, and this place is not suited to your comfort. Come with me to the hut on the mountain. The sun is still high; before it sets behind the snowy peaks and shines on another land, you will have heard all I have to say. Then, the choice will be yours—either I will leave mankind forever and live in peace, or I will unleash my misery upon the world and be the cause of your own destruction."

With that, he turned and walked across the ice. I hesitated, then followed. My heart was heavy, and I said nothing, but as I walked, I thought about his words. At the very least, I needed to know the truth. Had he really killed my brother? I needed to be sure. For the first time, I began to consider what my responsibility was to the creature I had created. Did I owe him happiness before I could blame him for his crimes? These thoughts convinced me to listen to his story.

We made our way across the icy ground and up the steep, rocky hillside. The freezing air bit at my skin, and soon, the rain started falling once more. At last, we reached a small hut. The creature entered with an air of victory, while I followed with a heavy heart, filled with fear and uncertainty. But I had given my word that I would listen. I sat down by the fire he had made, its warmth doing little to ease my discomfort, and braced myself for the story he was about to tell.

Chapter 11

I struggled to remember the first moments of my life; everything from that time felt unclear and confusing. I was suddenly overwhelmed by many different sensations—I could see, hear, touch, and smell all at once. At first, I couldn't tell them apart. Over time, I began to understand them little by little. A bright light hurt my eyes, so I shut them. The darkness confused me, but as soon as I opened my eyes again, the light returned. I started to move and walk, though I wasn't sure where I was going. Before, I had been surrounded by solid things that I couldn't see through, but now I could move freely without anything blocking my path.

The light became too much for me, and the heat exhausted me as I walked. I looked for shade and found a forest near Ingolstadt. There, I lay down by a small stream, resting until hunger and thirst forced me to move again. I found some berries hanging from trees and lying on the ground, eating them to ease my hunger. I drank from the brook, and soon, sleep overtook me.

When I woke up, it was dark, and I felt cold and afraid. I was completely alone. Before I left your home, I had covered myself with some clothes because I had felt cold, but they weren't enough to protect me from the damp night air. I was weak, helpless, and miserable. I didn't understand anything around me, but I knew I was in pain, and I began to cry.

Soon, a soft light appeared in the sky, and I felt a strange sense of comfort. I stood up and saw a glowing shape rise from behind the trees—it was the moon. I watched it with wonder as it moved slowly across the sky, lighting my way. I searched for more berries and, while wandering, found a large cloak under a tree. I wrapped myself in it and sat on the ground. My mind was full of jumbled thoughts. I could feel the light, hunger, thirst, and darkness, and I heard endless sounds around me. The only thing I could clearly recognize was the bright moon, and I stared at it with pleasure.

Many days and nights passed, and the moon grew smaller. I slowly began to understand my surroundings. I could now clearly see the clear stream where I drank and the trees that shaded me. I felt joy when I realized that the pleasant sounds I often heard came from the small winged creatures—birds—that sometimes blocked the light from my eyes. I started to notice the shapes of things around me and could see the sky stretching above me. I tried to copy the sweet songs of the birds, but I couldn't. I wanted to make my own sounds to express how I felt, but the noises that came from me were strange and rough, scaring me into silence.

The moon disappeared for a time and returned, smaller each night. By then, my senses had become clearer, and I was learning more every day. My eyes got used to the light, and I could now recognize objects. I could tell the difference between insects and plants, and over time, I learned to distinguish one plant from another. I noticed that some birds had harsh, unpleasant calls, while others, like blackbirds and thrushes, sang beautiful melodies.

One day, while I was shivering from the cold, I found a fire left behind by wandering travelers. The warmth was wonderful, and I was filled with joy. Curious, I reached out and placed my hand in the glowing embers, but the sudden pain made me cry out and pull back immediately. I was shocked that something could bring both comfort and pain. I examined the fire carefully and realized it was made of wood. Excited, I gathered some sticks and tried to add them to the flames, but they were too wet and wouldn't burn. Frustrated, I sat and watched, trying to understand. I noticed that the heat dried out the wet wood, and once dry, the branches caught fire. I repeated this process, gathering as much wood as I could to keep a steady supply for the fire.

As night fell, I feared the fire would go out while I slept. To protect it, I carefully covered it with dry wood and leaves, placing damp branches nearby so they would dry overnight. Then, I wrapped myself in my cloak, lay on the ground, and drifted into sleep.

When I woke up in the morning, my first thought was to check the fire. I carefully uncovered it, and a light breeze caused the embers to glow and burst into flames again. I learned from this and created a fan of branches to revive the fire whenever it started to die. As night fell once more, I realized that the fire not only kept me warm but also gave light in the darkness. I also discovered another use for it—when I ate some food left behind by the travelers, I noticed that some of it had been roasted and tasted much better than the berries I had been eating. I decided to cook my own food in the fire, placing different things on the embers to see how they changed. The berries were ruined, but nuts and roots became softer and more flavorful. This discovery filled me with excitement, as I had found a new way to survive.

Food became harder to find, and I often spent the entire day searching for just a few acorns to ease my hunger. Realizing how difficult it was to survive there, I decided to leave and search for a better place where my basic needs would be easier to meet. However, I deeply regretted losing the fire I had found by accident, since I didn't know how to create it myself. I spent hours trying to figure out a way to make fire again, but I failed. Wrapping myself in my cloak, I set off through the woods, walking toward the setting sun.

For three days, I wandered. At last, I reached the open countryside. Snow had fallen the night before, covering the ground in a thick, unbroken white layer. The sight was bleak, and the cold wetness of the snow numbed my feet.

It was early in the morning, and I desperately wanted food and shelter. Finally, I spotted a small hut on a small hill. It seemed to be built for a shepherd, and I examined it with great curiosity. When I found the door open, I stepped inside. An old man was sitting near a fire, preparing his breakfast. As soon as he heard me enter, he turned, let out a loud cry, and ran from the hut as fast as he could, surprising me with his speed despite his frail body. His appearance was unlike anything I had ever seen before, and his reaction startled me.

Still, I was overjoyed by the hut itself. Inside, I was protected from the cold, wind, and rain. The floor was dry, and compared to the misery of being outside, this place felt like paradise. I quickly ate the leftovers of the shepherd's meal—bread, cheese, milk, and wine. However, I did not like the wine. Exhausted, I lay down on some straw and fell into a deep sleep.

When I woke up at noon, the bright sunlight reflecting off the snow made the air feel warmer. Drawn by the warmth, I decided to continue my journey. Before leaving, I packed the rest of the shepherd's food in a small bag I had found. I walked across the fields for several hours, and by sunset, I reached a village. The sight amazed me. The houses— some simple huts, others neat cottages, and even a few large buildings—filled me with wonder. I saw gardens with vegetables, and I spotted milk and cheese sitting on the windowsills of some homes. My hunger grew stronger.

I entered one of the better-looking houses, but the moment I stepped inside, the children screamed in terror, and one of the women fainted. The entire village erupted in chaos—some people ran, while others attacked me. I was hit by stones and other objects, suffering painful blows, until I finally managed to escape. Terrified and injured, I fled into the open countryside.

I took shelter in a small, shabby hut. Compared to the village homes, it was miserable, but it was at least a place to hide. The hut was connected to a much nicer cottage, but after my terrible experience in the village, I did not dare to go near it. My shelter was small, made of wood, and so low that I could barely sit upright. The floor was simply dirt, but at least it was dry. Although cold wind slipped through the many cracks, I was grateful for the protection it provided from the snow and rain.

I settled in, relieved to have found a place to stay, no matter how poor. But even more than the cold, I was grateful to be hidden from the cruelty of humans. When morning came, I crawled out of my shelter to observe the nearby cottage and see if I could remain where I was. My hiding place was built right against the back of the cottage, and on one side, there was a pigsty and a small clear pool of water. One part of the hut was open, which was how I had entered. I used stones and wood to cover the gaps so that I wouldn't be seen, but I left a small opening that I could move when I needed to go in and out. The pigsty let in enough light for me, so I was satisfied with my hiding spot.

Now that my shelter was secure, I turned my attention to survival. I had managed to take a loaf of rough bread, which I ate for breakfast, and I found a cup to drink from the pool more easily. The ground inside my hut was slightly raised, keeping it dry, and since it was close to the cottage's chimney, it stayed warmer than I expected. Compared to the freezing, wet forest where I had lived before, this place felt like a paradise.

After eating, I was about to remove a plank to fetch water when I heard footsteps. Through a small gap, I saw a young girl carrying a pail on her head as she walked past my hiding place. She was different from other villagers I had seen—she had a gentle, patient look, though she also seemed sad. Her clothing was simple, just a rough blue skirt and a plain linen jacket. Her fair hair was braided, though without any decorations.

I watched as she disappeared from view, then returned about fifteen minutes later with the pail now partly filled with milk. As she struggled with the weight of it, a young man approached her. His face showed even greater sorrow. He spoke a few words to her, took the heavy pail from her head, and carried it to the cottage. She followed him inside. A short while later, I saw the young man again, this time carrying tools as he walked across the field behind the cottage. The girl also busied herself, moving between the house and the yard. I continued to watch, curious about their lives and whether I could safely remain hidden near them.

As I examined my shelter, I discovered that it had once been part of the cottage. A window had been covered with wood, but there was a tiny crack that allowed me to peek inside. Through this small opening, I could see a simple, clean room with very little furniture. In one corner, near a small fire, sat an old man with silver hair. He rested his head in his hands, looking sad and deep in thought.

The young girl was busy tidying up the cottage, but soon she took something out of a drawer and sat beside the old man. He picked up a strange instrument and began to play, producing sounds even more beautiful than the songs of birds. The melody was soft and sorrowful, and I noticed tears falling from the young girl's eyes. At first, the old man did not seem to notice, but when she began to sob, he spoke a few gentle words. She immediately left her work and knelt at his feet. He lifted her up with a kind smile, full of love and warmth.

Watching this scene, I felt something new, something I had never experienced before. It was a mixture of joy and sadness, a strange and overwhelming feeling that had nothing to do with hunger, cold, or warmth. Unable to bear these emotions, I pulled away from the window.

A little while later, the young man returned, carrying a heavy bundle of wood on his shoulders. The girl met him at the door and helped him unload it. She took some of the wood inside and placed it on the fire. Then, the young man showed her a large loaf of bread and a piece of cheese, and she smiled. She went into the garden, picked some roots and herbs, and placed them in water before setting them over the fire to cook. Afterward, she went back to her tasks inside, while the young man stayed outside, digging in the garden and pulling up more plants. After an hour, the girl joined him, and they walked back into the cottage together.

While they worked, the old man sat quietly, lost in thought. But when they came back inside, he brightened up and joined them for a meal. They ate quickly, and then the young woman resumed her chores, while the old man stepped outside for a short walk in the sunlight, leaning on the young man's arm. The contrast between them was striking—the older man, frail but full of warmth and kindness, and the younger man, graceful but weighed down with sadness. After a few minutes, the old man returned to the cottage, while the young man grabbed a different set of tools and headed out across the fields.

Night fell quickly, but to my surprise, the cottagers did not immediately go to sleep. They lit candles, keeping the room bright even after the sun had set. I was pleased to see that I could continue watching them even in the darkness. In the evening, the young girl and the young man worked on tasks I didn't understand, while the old man picked up his instrument again and played the beautiful music that had enchanted me earlier in the day. When he finished, the young man began speaking—not singing or playing, but making steady, rhythmic sounds. At the time, I did not know what he was doing, but later I learned that he was reading aloud. Back then, I knew nothing about words or letters, so I did not understand what was happening.

After a short while, they put out their candles and, as I guessed, went to bed.

Chapter 12

I lay on my straw bed, unable to sleep, my thoughts consumed by everything I had witnessed that day. What struck me the most was the kindness and gentleness of the cottagers. I longed to be part of their world, but fear held me back. The memory of how the villagers had treated me the night before was still fresh in my mind. I knew I had to stay hidden, at least for now. Instead, I would watch them from my shelter, observing their behavior and trying to understand what influenced their actions.

The next morning, the cottagers woke up before sunrise. The young woman tidied up the cottage and prepared breakfast, while the young man left after their meal.

That day was much like the one before. The young man worked outside, while the girl stayed busy with chores inside. The old man, whom I soon realized was blind, spent his time playing his instrument or sitting in deep thought. I was touched by how much love and respect the younger cottagers showed him. They cared for him with great kindness, and he rewarded them with warm smiles.

Still, they did not seem completely happy. The young man and the girl would sometimes sit together and cry, though I didn't understand why. They had a warm home, food to eat, and clothes to wear. Most importantly, they had each other's company, sharing kind words and affectionate looks. I wondered what could make them sad. If such good and beautiful people could be unhappy, then it made sense that I, lonely and different, should feel miserable too. But I wanted to understand their sorrow, and as time passed, I learned more about them.

Eventually, I realized that their sadness came from poverty. They struggled to get enough food, especially during the winter when their cow gave very little milk. I often saw the young man and the girl give their portions to the old man, keeping nothing for themselves.

This act of selflessness moved me deeply. Up until then, I had been secretly taking small amounts of their food at night to feed myself. But when I realized that my actions were making their lives harder, I stopped. Instead, I survived on berries, nuts, and roots from the nearby forest.

I also found another way to help them. I saw that the young man spent much of his time gathering firewood for the family. At night, I took his tools and collected wood myself, leaving enough to last for days.

The first time I did this, the young woman was shocked when she stepped outside in the morning and saw the pile of wood. She called for the young man, who also looked surprised. I was pleased to see that he did not have to go into the cold forest that day. Instead, he spent his time repairing the cottage and working in the garden.

As time went on, I made an even greater discovery. I realized that these people could communicate their thoughts and feelings to each other using spoken words. The sounds they made could bring happiness or sadness, comfort or distress. This ability to express themselves fascinated me, and I longed to understand it. But at first, I struggled. Their speech was too fast, and I could not figure out what the words meant.

Still, I kept listening, and after many weeks, I began to recognize the names of simple things. I learned the words for fire, milk, bread, and wood. Then, I discovered the names of the cottagers. The young man and the girl had several names, but the old man was always called "father." The girl was called "sister" or "Agatha," and the young man was called "Felix," "brother," or "son." The joy I felt when I finally understood these words was indescribable. I also picked up a few other words, like "good," "dearest," and "unhappy," though I did not yet fully understand their meaning.

I spent the winter this way, quietly observing and learning from the cottagers. Their kindness and grace made me care for them deeply. When they were sad, I felt sorrow too. When they were happy, I shared in their joy. These were the only people I had ever known, and I admired them.

I rarely saw any other humans, but on the rare occasions that visitors came to the cottage, they seemed rough and unfriendly compared to my cottagers. The old man often tried to lift his children's spirits. He spoke gently to them, and though Agatha sometimes wiped away tears, she always seemed more cheerful afterward. But Felix was different. He was the saddest of them all. Even though his voice was warm when he spoke to his father, I could tell he had suffered more than anyone else.

I could recall many small moments that showed how kind and caring the cottagers were. Even though they lived in poverty, Felix was always thoughtful. He happily brought Agatha the first little white flower that peeked through the snow. Early each morning, before she woke up, he cleared the snow from her path to the milk-house, fetched water from the well, and carried wood inside. He was always surprised to find the woodpile mysteriously restocked. During the day, he often left for work, sometimes returning at midday without any wood, which made me think he worked for a nearby farmer. When he stayed home, he helped in the garden, but since there was little work to do in the winter, he spent much of his time reading to Agatha and their father.

At first, I was confused by the way Felix read aloud, but soon I realized that the sounds he made when reading were similar to those he used when speaking. I figured out that the marks on the paper must be symbols for words. I desperately wanted to understand this, but how could I learn to read when I didn't even know the meaning of many spoken words? Still, I paid close attention, and though I wasn't able to follow full conversations, I made progress. I knew that if I ever wanted to reveal myself to the cottagers, I needed to speak their language first. I hoped that if they could understand me, they might look past my terrifying appearance.

I had admired how graceful and beautiful they were, but when I saw my own reflection in a clear pool of water, I was horrified. At first, I recoiled, unable to believe that the hideous creature staring back at me was really myself. But when I accepted the truth, I felt deep sadness and shame. I had yet to fully understand how much my appearance would shape my fate.

As the days grew longer and the air became warmer, the snow melted, revealing the bare trees and dark earth beneath. Felix became busier, and the signs of hunger in the household faded. Their food was simple but enough to sustain them, and more plants began growing in the garden. As the weather improved, I often saw the old man take walks with Felix's help. I learned that when rain fell from the sky, it was called "rain." It happened often, but strong winds would dry the ground quickly, making the season feel more pleasant.

My life in the small shelter remained the same each day. In the mornings, I watched the cottagers, and when they went about their work, I would sleep. Later in the day, I observed them again, learning from their actions. At night, if there was moonlight or a clear sky, I would go into the woods to gather food for myself and firewood for the family. Whenever needed, I would also clear the snow from their path, just as I had seen Felix do. They were amazed by these unseen acts of kindness, and I once heard them call it the work of a "good spirit" or "something wonderful," though I didn't yet understand those words.

I grew more curious about these people, wanting to understand their emotions. Why was Felix so sad? Why did Agatha seem troubled? I foolishly thought that maybe I could help them find happiness. Even when I slept, I dreamed of them—the wise old father, the kind Agatha, and the noble Felix. I imagined them as higher beings, the ones who would decide my fate. Over and over, I pictured the moment I would reveal myself to them. At first, they would be afraid of my appearance, but I hoped that through kindness and gentle words, I could earn their trust and love.

These thoughts gave me hope and made me work harder to learn their language. My voice was rough, not soft like theirs, but I managed to pronounce the words I had learned with some effort. I felt like a clumsy animal trying to fit into a world of grace, but I believed that my good intentions should count more than my awkward nature.

With spring came warm rains and bright sunshine, and the world around me changed. People who had stayed inside during the harsh winter now appeared, tending to their fields and working the land. The birds sang more joyfully, and fresh green leaves sprouted on the trees. The world looked like a paradise, a place fit for gods, completely different from the cold and lifeless season before. The beauty of nature filled me with happiness, pushing away memories of my past suffering. In that moment, I felt peace, and I dared to hope that my future would bring joy.

Chapter 13

I now hurry to the most important part of my story, the events that changed me forever.

Spring arrived quickly, bringing warm weather and clear skies. I was amazed at how the once gloomy, empty land had transformed into a place full of life, covered in green grass and beautiful flowers. The fresh scents and bright colors filled me with joy.

One day, as the cottagers took a break from their daily work, the old man played his guitar while the others listened. Felix, however, looked sadder than ever. He sighed often, and at one point, his father paused his music to ask him what was wrong. Felix answered in a cheerful voice, but his expression remained sorrowful. Just then, there was a knock at the door.

A woman on horseback had arrived, accompanied by a man who appeared to be her guide. She wore dark clothing and a thick black veil that covered her face. Agatha spoke to her, but instead of answering, the stranger simply said Felix's name in a soft, musical voice. Though her voice was beautiful, it sounded different from that of the cottagers. The moment Felix heard her, he rushed toward her. As soon as she saw him, she lifted her veil, revealing an incredibly beautiful face. She had dark, shiny hair, gentle yet lively eyes, and perfect features. Her skin was fair, and her cheeks had a lovely pink glow.

Felix's sadness disappeared instantly. His face lit up with happiness, and his eyes sparkled with joy. He looked as delighted as the young woman was beautiful. She, however, seemed more emotional. She wiped away a few tears, then held out her hand. Felix eagerly kissed it and called her his "sweet Arabian," though she didn't seem to understand his words. Instead, she smiled. He helped her off the horse, sent her guide away, and led her into the cottage. He spoke with his father, and the young woman knelt at the old man's feet, trying to kiss his hand. Instead, he gently lifted her up and embraced her warmly.

I soon realized that, although she could speak, she didn't understand the cottagers' language, nor did they understand hers. They tried to communicate through gestures, which I couldn't quite understand, but it was clear that her arrival brought happiness to the home. Felix, especially, was overjoyed. His usual sadness disappeared, and he welcomed her with smiles. Agatha, ever gentle, kissed the young woman's hands and made gestures that seemed to say Felix had been sad before she arrived. The cottage was filled with a happiness I hadn't seen before, though I didn't yet understand the reason.

After some time, I noticed that the stranger was trying to learn their language. She repeated certain words they said, and I suddenly had an idea—I could learn along with her! She learned about twenty words that day, some of which I already knew, but I eagerly memorized the new ones.

As night fell, Agatha and the stranger went to bed early. Before they parted, Felix kissed the young woman's hand and said, "Good night, sweet Safie." I listened as Felix stayed up late talking with his father, and since I heard the name "Safie" many times, I realized that must be the woman's name. I wanted desperately to understand their conversation, but it was still impossible.

The next morning, Felix left for work, and after Agatha finished her usual tasks, Safie sat by the old man and picked up his guitar. She played so beautifully that I was completely enchanted. Her music was so moving that it brought tears to my eyes, filling me with both joy and sorrow. Then she began to sing, her voice rising and falling like a nightingale in the woods.

When she finished, she handed the guitar to Agatha, who hesitated at first. Eventually, she played a simple tune and sang along in a soft, sweet voice. It was lovely, but not as breathtaking as Safie's song. The old man looked overjoyed and spoke words that Agatha tried to explain to Safie. He seemed to be telling her how much he loved her music.

Life in the cottage continued as before, but now, instead of sadness, there was happiness. Safie was always cheerful, and she and I both improved quickly in learning the language. Within two months, I could understand most of what my cottagers said.

During this time, the earth transformed once more. The once dark ground was now covered in fresh green grass, and wildflowers bloomed everywhere, spreading sweet scents through the air. At night, they shone like tiny stars in the moonlit woods. The sun grew warmer, the nights became gentle and cool, and my nighttime walks became even more enjoyable. However, because the sun set later and rose earlier, I had less time to roam. I never dared to go out during the day, still afraid that if people saw me, they would treat me the same way they had in the first village I visited.

I spent my days carefully listening so I could learn the language faster. I was proud to realize that I was learning more quickly than Safie, who still struggled to speak fluently. I, on the other hand, could understand almost everything the cottagers said and could repeat their words with ease.

As I learned to speak, I also began to understand written language. Felix was teaching Safie how to read, and I paid close attention to his lessons. This opened up a whole new world to me, filling me with both amazement and excitement.

The book Felix used to teach Safie was called Ruins of Empires by Volney. I wouldn't have understood it on my own, but Felix explained it carefully as he read. He chose this book because its dramatic style was similar to the writing of Eastern authors. Through it, I learned about history and the great empires that once ruled the world. I discovered how different people lived, their governments, and their beliefs. I heard about the laziness of some cultures, the intelligence and creativity of the Greeks, the bravery and discipline of the early Romans, and how their once-great empire eventually fell. I learned about knights, kings, and the rise of Christianity. I also heard about the discovery of America and, like Safie, felt deep sadness for the suffering of the native people.

These stories stirred strange emotions in me. Humans could be powerful, noble, and full of goodness, yet also cruel and evil. Sometimes they seemed godlike, and at other times, they acted worse than animals. I came to believe that being a good and honorable person was the greatest achievement one could reach. But to be wicked was the lowest possible state, worse than that of a blind mole or a simple worm. At first, I couldn't understand why humans hurt one another or why there were laws and rulers. But as I learned more about crime and war, I became disgusted and saddened by the reality of human nature.

Every conversation in the cottage taught me something new. As Felix helped Safie understand the world, I also learned. I heard about wealth and poverty, about social classes, and how people were judged based on their birth and status.

This made me think about myself. I realized that people valued noble birth and riches above all else. Some were respected even if they had only one of these things, but those who had neither were often treated as outcasts, forced to work for the benefit of the privileged few.

And what was I? I had no idea where I came from or who had created me. I had no money, no family, no home. On top of that, I looked hideous. I wasn't even like the humans I watched—I was stronger, could survive on little food, and endured extreme heat and cold without much harm. I was also much taller than them. As I looked around, I saw no one else like me. Was I truly a monster? A creature so unnatural that everyone feared and rejected me?

The more I thought about this, the more miserable I became. I wanted to forget these thoughts, but my sadness only grew with my understanding of the world. How I wished I had never left the woods where I was born! If only I had remained ignorant, only feeling hunger, thirst, and warmth!

Knowledge is a strange thing. Once it takes hold of your mind, it never lets go, clinging to you like moss on a rock. Sometimes, I wanted to stop thinking and feeling altogether, but I learned that there was only one way to escape pain—death. I feared it, but I did not understand it.

I loved goodness and admired the kind-hearted cottagers. But I was an outsider, only able to watch them in secret. I longed to be part of their lives, but I could not. I wanted to hear Agatha's gentle words and see Safie's bright smile directed at me. I wanted to listen to the wise advice of the old man and share in Felix's lively conversations. But those things were not meant for me. I was alone.

I learned even more about human life. I heard about the difference between men and women, how children were born, and how families were filled with love. I listened to stories of fathers who cherished their children and mothers who gave their entire hearts to raising them. I learned how siblings grew together, bound by deep connections of love and loyalty.

But where was my family? Who had loved me as a child? No father had guided me, no mother had smiled at me. If I had ever known such things, my past was now a blank, an empty space with no memories. From my very first moment of awareness, I had been as I was now—fully grown, alone, and different from everyone else. I had never met another being like me, nor had anyone ever claimed me as their own.

What was I? I kept asking myself this question, but the only answer was sorrow.

I will soon explain where these thoughts led me. But first, let me return to the cottagers, whose story filled me with so many emotions—anger, happiness, and wonder. In the end, all these feelings only deepened my love and admiration for them. In my mind, I thought of them as my protectors, though they did not even know I existed.

Chapter 14

It took some time before I learned the full story of the cottagers. Their past was both fascinating and tragic, and every detail was new and surprising to me.

The old man's name was De Lacey. He came from a respected family in France and had once lived a comfortable life, admired by those around him. His son, Felix, had trained to serve his country, and Agatha had been part of high society. Just months before my arrival, they had lived in a grand city called Paris, surrounded by friends and enjoying the kind of happiness that comes from intelligence, virtue, and a modest but sufficient fortune.

Their downfall was caused by Safie's father. He was a wealthy Turkish merchant who had lived in Paris for many years, but for reasons I could not fully understand, the government saw him as a threat. He was arrested and thrown into prison on the very same day that Safie arrived from Constantinople to be with him. He was soon put on trial and sentenced to death. The trial was unfair, and many people in Paris were outraged. It seemed clear that he had been condemned not because of any real crime, but because of his religion and wealth.

Felix happened to be in the courtroom during the trial. He was horrified by the unjust sentence and, in that moment, vowed to rescue the man. He searched for a way into the prison and eventually discovered a grated window in an unguarded part of the building. Through it, he saw the prisoner, weighed down by chains, waiting helplessly for his execution. Late at night, Felix returned and spoke to the man, revealing his plan to save him. The Turk, shocked but overjoyed, tried to win Felix's loyalty by offering him money and great rewards. Felix refused these gifts, but when he saw Safie visiting her father and expressing her gratitude with kind gestures, his heart was deeply moved. The prisoner had something far more valuable than riches—his beautiful daughter.

The Turk quickly noticed Felix's growing affection for Safie. Wanting to secure his own escape, he promised that Felix could marry her as soon as he was safely out of France. Though Felix was too honorable to openly accept this deal, the idea of marrying Safie gave him even more motivation to succeed.

As the escape plan moved forward, Safie sent letters to Felix. With the help of an old servant who knew French, she wrote heartfelt messages thanking him for trying to save her father. At the same time, she shared her own sadness about her situation.

I found these letters during my time in the hovel, as Felix and Agatha often read them. I even gathered materials to write them down, and before I leave, I will give them to you as proof of my story. But for now, I will only summarize their contents, as the sun is already beginning to set.

Safie's letters revealed that her mother had been a Christian Arab who was captured and enslaved by the Turks. Because of her beauty, she caught the eye of Safie's father, who married her. Safie spoke about her mother with deep admiration. She had been born free and resented the life of servitude she was forced into. Despite this, she raised her daughter with strong values, teaching her about her faith and encouraging her to seek knowledge and independence—things that were not allowed for most women in her culture.

Though Safie's mother passed away, her lessons remained in her daughter's heart. Safie was horrified by the idea of returning to the East, where she would be locked away in a harem, forced to spend her life in meaningless amusements that went against her intelligence and spirit. She longed to marry a Christian and live in a place where women had rights and could be respected in society.

The day of the Turk's execution was set, but before it could take place, he escaped from prison. By the next morning, he was far from Paris. Felix had secretly obtained travel documents for himself, his father, and his sister. Before the escape, he told his father of his plan, and De Lacey helped by leaving his home under the pretense of a journey. He and Agatha hid in an unknown part of Paris.

Felix then led Safie and her father out of France. They traveled through the countryside to Lyons, then crossed the mountains into Italy, where they stopped in the city of Leghorn. There, the Turk planned to wait for the right moment to return to his homeland.

Safie had no intention of leaving without Felix. Her father reassured her that she would be allowed to marry him once they were safe. Felix stayed with them, looking forward to the day they could be together. In the meantime, he and Safie spent as much time as possible together, their feelings for each other growing stronger. They spoke with the help of a translator, but often, words weren't even needed. Safie would sing to Felix, her voice carrying the beautiful melodies of her homeland.

The Turk acted as if he approved of their relationship, even encouraging their growing bond. But in secret, he had other plans. The idea of his daughter marrying a Christian disgusted him. However, he knew Felix was still dangerous—if he angered him, Felix could turn him over to the Italian authorities. So, the Turk pretended to support the match while secretly plotting a way to take Safie with him when he left.

His chance came when troubling news arrived from Paris.

The French government was furious when they discovered that their prisoner had escaped. They did everything they could to track down and punish the person responsible. It didn't take long for them to uncover Felix's involvement, and soon, his father, De Lacey, and his sister, Agatha, were thrown into prison.

When Felix heard the news, his happiness vanished. The thought of his blind, elderly father and kind sister suffering in a filthy prison while he was free and with the woman he loved was unbearable. He quickly made an agreement with Safie's father: if the Turk found a way to escape before Felix could return, Safie would stay at a convent in Leghorn until he came back for her. Then, without hesitation, Felix left Safie behind and turned himself in to the authorities in Paris, hoping that by surrendering, he could secure the release of his family.

But his plan failed. De Lacey and Agatha remained in prison for five long months before their trial. When the case was finally decided, they lost all their wealth and were permanently banished from France. With nowhere else to go, they found shelter in the small cottage in Germany, which was where I first discovered them.

Felix then learned of the ultimate betrayal. The Turkish merchant, the very man for whom he and his family had sacrificed everything, had abandoned them. After realizing that Felix had lost his status and money, the Turk decided he no longer had to honor his promise. Instead of showing gratitude, he fled Italy with his daughter, leaving behind only a small sum of money as an insulting token to "help Felix start over."

This act of selfishness and betrayal broke Felix's heart. He could have endured poverty, even accepted exile, if it had been for a noble cause. But losing Safie and realizing the man he had risked everything for had turned his back on him was unbearable. When Safie finally arrived, it was like life had returned to him.

Back in Leghorn, when the Turk heard that Felix had lost his fortune and title, he ordered his daughter to forget about him and prepare to return to her homeland. But Safie was outraged. She tried to reason with her father, but he became angry and refused to listen.

A few days later, the Turk entered Safie's room in a hurry. He told her he had learned that the French government was after him and that he would be arrested soon. He had arranged for a ship to take him to Constantinople, and he would be leaving in just a few hours. He planned for Safie to stay behind with a trusted servant and follow him later, bringing the rest of his fortune that had not yet arrived in Leghorn.

Left alone, Safie made a decision. She had no desire to live in Turkey, where she would be confined and treated as a lesser person because of her gender and beliefs. As she was looking through her father's papers, she discovered news of Felix's exile and learned the name of the place where he now lived. She hesitated for a while but finally made up her mind.

Gathering a few of her valuable jewels and some money, she left Italy with a servant who was from Leghorn but could also speak the basic language of Turkey. Together, they set off for Germany in search of Felix.

Safie traveled safely for most of the journey, but when they were about twenty leagues away from De Lacey's cottage, her servant became gravely ill. Safie cared for her with love and dedication, but sadly, the woman did not survive. Now, Safie was completely alone, unable to speak the language and unfamiliar with the customs of the country.

Luckily, she found kind people who helped her. Before her servant died, she had told someone the name of the place they were headed. After her passing, the woman who had taken them in made sure that Safie safely reached the cottage where Felix and his family were staying.

Chapter 15

The story of the cottagers left a deep impression on me. Through them, I saw the goodness people were capable of, but I also became aware of human cruelty and injustice.

At that time, I still thought of crime as something distant, something that did not concern me. All I saw was kindness and generosity, which made me eager to take part in the world and experience these things for myself. But before I continue explaining how my mind developed, I must tell you about something important that happened in early August that year.

One night, while I was in the forest gathering food and firewood, I came across a small leather bag lying on the ground. Inside, I found some clothing and a few books. I was thrilled with this discovery and hurried back to my shelter. The books were written in the same language I had been learning from the cottagers, so I could read them. They were Paradise Lost, Plutarch's Lives, and The Sorrows of Werter. These books became my greatest treasures, and I spent every spare moment studying them while the cottagers went about their daily lives.

It is difficult to describe the effect these books had on me. They filled my mind with new ideas and emotions. At times, I felt incredible joy, but more often, I sank into deep sadness. The Sorrows of Werter moved me with its simple but heartbreaking story. The book explored so many ideas and explained things that had once been confusing to me. I was drawn to the way it described love, longing, and sadness, and I found myself admiring Werter as if he were a real person. His words about life and death made me wonder about these things myself. I did not fully understand them, but I mourned his fate, even without knowing exactly why.

As I read, I saw pieces of myself in the characters, yet I also felt like I did not belong among them. I could understand their emotions, but I was different from them in every way. I had no family, no connections, no one to care for me. I was alone in the world, with nothing to lose. My reflection was hideous, my size unnatural. What did this mean? Who was I? Where had I come from? Why was I here? These questions haunted me, but I could not find any answers.

Plutarch's Lives affected me in a different way. Unlike Werter, which made me feel hopeless, this book lifted my spirits. It told the stories of great leaders, warriors, and lawgivers who shaped the world. I had never known about governments, empires, or great battles. The cottagers had been my only glimpse into human society, but this book showed me a much larger world. I admired the wise and peaceful leaders the most—men like Numa, Solon, and Lycurgus—rather than conquerors like Romulus and Theseus. Perhaps if I had first learned about humanity from a soldier seeking glory, I might have developed different values. But because of the cottagers, I respected kindness and wisdom above all else.

Paradise Lost, however, stirred something deeper in me. I read it as if it were a real history, not just a story. It filled me with awe and fear to see how God, the all-powerful creator, fought against his own creations. I often compared myself to Adam, who, like me, seemed to have no connection to others. But Adam had been created perfect, loved, and cared for by his maker. He was given knowledge and companionship. I, on the other hand, was miserable, abandoned, and alone. More often, I felt like Satan—cast out, watching others enjoy happiness while I was filled with envy and sorrow.

Then, something happened that deepened these feelings even more. When I first arrived at the hovel, I had found some papers in the pocket of the clothing I had taken from your laboratory. At the time, I could not read them, but now that I understood the language, I finally studied them. They were your notes—the detailed record of how you had created me. You described every step of my construction, every moment leading up to my birth. You wrote of my appearance with such disgust that I could feel your horror as if it were my own.

I felt sick as I read. I cursed the day I was given life. "Hateful day!" I cried in agony. "Cursed creator! Why did you make me so ugly that even you could not bear to look at me? God made man in his own image, beautiful and perfect. But I am a twisted, hideous version of you—worse because I resemble you yet am nothing like you. Even Satan had other fallen angels to share his suffering, but I am completely alone, despised by all."

These thoughts tormented me whenever I was alone. But when I watched the cottagers and saw their kindness, I allowed myself to hope. I believed that if they knew how much I admired them, they would take pity on me. Would they truly turn me away just because of my appearance, if I approached them with nothing but kindness and a plea for friendship? I told myself not to lose hope.

Still, I was afraid. I knew that how they reacted to me would determine my fate. I decided to wait and prepare myself before revealing my existence. I wanted to be certain that I could communicate with them properly. My understanding of their language improved every day, so I chose to wait a little longer, hoping that with time, I would be even more ready.

As time passed, things changed in the cottage. Safie's presence filled the home with happiness, and I noticed that they had more food and comfort than before. Felix and Agatha spent more time talking and enjoying themselves, and they now had servants to help with their work. They were not rich, but they were content. Their lives were peaceful, while mine became more troubled with each passing day. The more I learned, the more I understood just how alone I truly was. I held onto hope, but it would disappear whenever I saw my reflection in the water or my shadow in the moonlight.

I tried to push away my fears and prepare myself for the moment I had been waiting for—the day I would finally reveal myself to the cottagers. Sometimes, I let my imagination run free, dreaming of kind and beautiful people who would welcome me, understand me, and ease my loneliness. But these were only dreams. I had no companion, no one to share my thoughts with. Even Adam had asked his creator for comfort, but who could I turn to? My own creator had abandoned me, and in my pain, I cursed him.

Autumn passed, and I watched with sadness as the leaves withered and fell. The trees became bare, and the world once again looked as bleak as it had when I first saw it. The cold did not bother me as much as the loss of the flowers, the singing birds, and the bright colors of summer. But the cottagers remained happy, unaffected by the change in seasons. Their love for one another never wavered. Seeing their joy only made me long even more to be a part of their lives. My greatest wish was to see them look at me with kindness, to feel like I belonged. I could not bear to think that they would see me as something horrible. They never turned away the poor who came to their door, so why should they reject me? I did not ask for food or shelter—I only wanted their compassion. I believed I was not completely unworthy of it.

Winter arrived, marking a full year since I had come to life. By this time, my only focus was my plan to introduce myself to the cottagers.

I thought carefully about how to do it. Eventually, I decided that my best chance was to approach the old man, De Lacey, while he was alone. I understood that my appearance was what frightened people the most. However, since De Lacey was blind, he could not judge me by my looks. My voice, though rough, was not frightening. I believed that if I could earn his trust and sympathy, he might help convince his children to accept me.

One afternoon, as golden sunlight shone on the fallen autumn leaves, Felix, Agatha, and Safie left for a long walk. De Lacey, wanting to rest, stayed home alone. I knew this was my chance. My heart pounded in my chest. This was the moment that would either bring me happiness or confirm my worst fears. The servants had gone to a nearby fair, and everything was quiet. It was the perfect opportunity. But as I stepped forward, my legs trembled, and I sank to the ground. After a moment, I gathered my strength, moved the wooden planks that hid my shelter, and stepped out into the fresh air. Determined, I made my way to the cottage.

I knocked on the door.

"Who is there?" De Lacey called. "Come in."

I entered. "Forgive me for disturbing you," I said. "I am a traveler in need of rest. Would you allow me to sit by your fire for a few minutes?"

"Of course," De Lacey replied. "I will help however I can, though I must warn you that my children are away. Since I am blind, I may not be able to provide much."

"Please, do not trouble yourself," I assured him. "I have food. All I need is warmth and a moment to rest."

I sat down, and for a while, there was silence. I knew every second mattered, but I did not know how to begin. Finally, De Lacey spoke.

"By your speech, I assume you are French. Are you from this country?"

"No," I answered, "but I was raised by a French family and learned their language. Now, I am on my way to seek the kindness of dear friends whom I love and hope will accept me."

"Are they German?" he asked.

"No, they are French," I replied. "But let's not talk about that for now. I am alone in this world. I have no family, no friends. These good people I wish to join have never seen me before. I fear that if they reject me, I will be an outcast forever."

"Do not lose hope," De Lacey said kindly. "It is truly sad to be without friends, but most people, when they are not blinded by selfishness, are full of kindness and goodwill. If your friends are good people, do not despair."

"They are the best people in the world," I said. "But they are prejudiced against me. I have done nothing wrong. My life has been harmless, and in some ways, I have even helped them. But they only see me as a monster."

"That is truly unfortunate," De Lacey said. "But if you have done nothing wrong, can you not prove it to them?"

"That is what I hope to do," I explained. "That is why I am so afraid. I care for these people deeply. For many months, I have secretly helped them in small ways, but they believe I mean them harm. It is this misunderstanding that I must correct."

"Where do these friends live?" he asked.

"Near this very place," I answered.

De Lacey was quiet for a moment, then said, "If you tell me your story, I may be able to help you. I cannot see your face, but your words seem sincere. I am poor and in exile myself, but if I can help another person, I will gladly do so."

I felt a rush of relief and gratitude. "You are truly kind," I said. "Your words give me hope. With your help, I believe I may finally be accepted."

"I hope so," he replied. "Even if you had done wrong, abandoning you would only lead you to despair. It would not help you become better. I, too, have suffered unfairly. My family and I were punished for a crime we did not commit. So, I understand your pain."

"How can I ever thank you?" I cried. "You are the first person to speak kindly to me. I will always be grateful to you. Your kindness gives me hope that my friends will accept me."

"May I ask who these friends are?" De Lacey inquired.

I hesitated. This was the moment that would decide my fate. I tried to gather my courage, but instead, I broke down. Overcome with emotion, I collapsed into a chair and sobbed. Just then, I heard footsteps outside. Felix, Agatha, and Safie had returned.

I had no time to waste. Desperately, I grabbed De Lacey's hand and pleaded, "Now is the moment! Please protect me! You and your family are the friends I seek. Do not turn me away!"

De Lacey gasped. "Great God! Who are you?"

At that moment, the door burst open. Felix, Safie, and Agatha stepped inside. Their faces twisted in horror as they saw me. Agatha fainted. Safie screamed and ran from the cottage. Felix, in a blind rage, rushed forward and tore me away from his father. With unnatural strength, he threw me to the ground and struck me with a stick.

I could have fought back. I was much stronger than Felix. I could have easily overpowered him. But my heart was crushed. My pain and sorrow were too great. I saw him lift his arm, ready to strike again. Instead of resisting, I turned and fled. Overwhelmed by misery, I escaped into the night, unseen by anyone.

Chapter 16

"Why did you create me, cursed maker? Why did I have to live? Why didn't I end my life the moment you forced me into this world? I don't know. At that moment, despair hadn't fully consumed me. Instead, I burned with rage and the desire for revenge. I wanted to tear down the cottage and destroy everyone inside. I longed to make them feel the pain I had suffered, to take satisfaction in their cries and misery."

That night, I left my hiding place and wandered deep into the woods. No longer afraid of being discovered, I howled in my grief like a wild beast. I ran through the trees with speed and fury, smashing anything that got in my way. Oh, what a terrible night it was! The cold stars seemed to mock me, and the bare trees swayed above, indifferent to my misery. Occasionally, the sweet sound of a bird's song pierced the silence, reminding me that the rest of the world was at peace while I burned with agony. I felt like a demon carrying my own personal hell inside me. I wanted to rip up the trees, destroy everything around me, and sit among the ruins, watching it all crumble.

But such rage could not last forever. My body grew weak from exhaustion, and I collapsed onto the cold, damp ground. There was not a single soul among the millions of people in the world who would care for me. So why should I care for them? No—I decided then and there that I would be at war with mankind for the rest of my existence. And above all, I swore revenge on the one who created me and cursed me with this unbearable misery.

When the sun rose, I heard voices in the distance and knew I could not return to my shelter while people were nearby. Instead, I hid in the thick brush, deciding to use the time to think about what had happened.

The warmth of the sun and the fresh air slowly calmed me. As I thought about what had taken place at the cottage, I began to realize that perhaps I had acted too quickly. It was true that I had made a mistake. The old man had seemed willing to accept me, and I had ruined everything by suddenly revealing myself to his family. I should have spent more time gaining his trust, allowing him to get used to me, and only then revealing myself to the others. But I still believed there was hope. After thinking for a long time, I decided I would return to the cottage and try to talk to the old man again. Perhaps he could still help me.

These thoughts brought me some peace, and by the afternoon, I fell into a deep sleep. But even in sleep, I found no rest. My mind was filled with images of the previous day—Agatha running away, Safie screaming, and Felix attacking me. I woke up exhausted, and by the time night fell, I was hungry. After finding food, I made my way back toward the cottage.

Everything was silent. I crept into my hiding place and waited for the family to wake up. But the usual time passed, and no one appeared. The sun rose high in the sky, yet the cottage remained dark and still. I trembled, afraid that something terrible had happened. I cannot describe the agony of waiting, unsure of what I would find.

Then, two men passed by, stopping near the cottage. They spoke to each other, waving their hands with strong gestures. But they spoke in a language different from the one my protectors used, so I could not understand them. Soon after, Felix arrived with another man. I was surprised because I knew he had not left the cottage that morning. I listened carefully, hoping to understand what was happening.

"Have you considered," the other man asked Felix, "that you will have to pay three months' rent and leave behind everything you've planted in the garden? I don't want to take advantage of you, so I suggest you take a few days to think it over."

"It's pointless," Felix replied. "We can never live here again. My father's health is in great danger because of what happened. My wife and sister will never recover from their fear. I beg you not to try to convince me otherwise. Take back your house—I must leave this place."

Felix's voice shook as he spoke. Then he and the other man entered the cottage for a few minutes before leaving again. That was the last time I ever saw the De Lacey family.

I spent the rest of the day in my shelter, lost in complete despair. My protectors had abandoned me, breaking the last connection I had to the world. For the first time, my heart was filled with hatred and the desire for revenge, and I made no effort to stop it. I let myself sink into my anger, my thoughts turning toward destruction. But when I remembered the kindness of De Lacey, the soft voice of Agatha, and the beauty of Safie, my rage faded for a moment, and I wept. Still, the pain of their rejection overwhelmed me. They had turned their backs on me, leaving me more alone than ever. My fury returned, and with no humans to take it out on, I turned my wrath toward the world itself.

As night fell, I gathered dry branches and anything else that would burn. I ripped up the plants from the garden and waited impatiently for the moon to sink lower in the sky.

Then the wind began to howl through the forest, tearing through the trees like a powerful storm. The sight and sound of it filled me with a wild energy, like I had lost all control of myself. I grabbed a burning branch from a tree and spun around in a furious dance, my eyes locked on the horizon. The moon had almost disappeared. I raised my torch high, watching the flames flicker. Then, with a loud scream, I set fire to the straw, the bushes, and the cottage itself.

The wind fanned the flames, and soon the entire house was burning, the fire consuming it with bright, twisting tongues.

Once I was sure nothing could save the cottage, I turned away and fled into the woods, seeking shelter.

Now that I had nowhere to go, where should I travel? I decided to leave this place behind, far away from the painful memories. But to me, every place in the world seemed just as terrible—I was hated everywhere. Then, I thought of you. I had learned from your notes that you were my creator, the one who had brought me to life. Who else should I turn to but the one responsible for my existence? Felix had taught Safie about geography, and I had listened carefully. From these lessons, I knew the locations of different places in the world. I also knew from your notes that Geneva was your hometown, so I decided to make my way there.

But how would I find my way? I knew I needed to travel southwest, but the sun was my only guide. I didn't know the names of the towns I would pass through, nor could I ask for directions from anyone. Still, I didn't lose hope. You were the only one I could turn to for help, though I felt nothing but hatred toward you. You had created me, given me the ability to feel and think, and then abandoned me, leaving me to be feared and hated by all. Yet you were the only person I had any right to ask for mercy. You were the only one I could seek justice from since no human would ever give it to me.

My journey was long and full of suffering. It was late autumn when I left the place I had been staying. I only traveled at night, afraid of being seen. Around me, nature was dying. The sun no longer gave warmth, rain and snow poured down, rivers froze, and the ground became hard and lifeless. I had no shelter. Oh, how often I cursed the day I was created! Any kindness I had once felt was gone, replaced by bitterness and anger. The closer I got to your home, the stronger my need for revenge grew. Snow fell, ice formed, but I didn't stop. I used a map I had found and followed whatever clues I could, though I often strayed off course. I was so consumed by rage and sorrow that nothing else mattered. But when I reached the borders of Switzerland, and the sun's warmth returned, a single event made my hatred even more powerful.

I usually hid during the day and traveled at night. But one morning, I found myself in a deep forest. Since the thick trees kept me hidden, I dared to continue my journey even after sunrise. It was one of the first days of spring, and the beauty of the sunlight and the fresh air filled me with an unexpected sense of peace. Feelings of joy, which I had thought were lost forever, stirred inside me. For a moment, I allowed myself to be happy. Tears rolled down my cheeks as I looked up at the bright sky, feeling thankful for the warmth it gave.

I wandered through the forest until I reached its edge, where a fast-moving river ran past the trees, their fresh green buds dipping into the water. I stopped, unsure which way to go, when I heard voices. Quickly, I hid behind a cypress tree. Soon, a young girl ran past, laughing as if she were playing a game with someone. She ran too close to the riverbank, slipped, and fell into the rushing water.

Without thinking, I rushed out from my hiding place. The current was strong, but I fought against it and pulled her to shore. She was unconscious, and I did everything I could to help her wake up. Just then, a man came running toward us—probably the one she had been playing with. The moment he saw me, he snatched the girl from my arms and carried her away into the woods. I followed him without knowing why. But as soon as he saw me getting closer, he aimed a gun at me and fired.

I collapsed in pain while he ran away into the trees.

This was my reward for showing kindness! I had saved a human life, and in return, I was shot. The pain of my wound was nothing compared to the hatred that burned inside me. My kindness had been met with violence, and now all the gentleness I had felt was gone. Pain turned into rage, and I swore that from that moment forward, I would hate all of humankind. But my suffering was too great, and my body weakened. I blacked out.

For weeks, I wandered through the forest, trying to heal. The bullet had pierced my shoulder, but I didn't know if it was still inside or had passed through. I had no way to treat my injury, no one to help me. But the worst pain came from knowing how cruel and unfair the world was. Every day, I made a vow: I would take my revenge, deep and terrible, to make up for the misery I had endured.

Eventually, my wound healed, and I continued my journey. But I could no longer find joy in the sunshine or the gentle breezes of spring. Happiness was a cruel joke, a reminder that I would never be part of it.

After two months of hardship, I finally reached the outskirts of Geneva.

It was evening when I arrived. I found a place to hide in the fields surrounding the city, thinking about how I should approach you. I was exhausted, starving, and too miserable to enjoy the beauty of the setting sun over the mountains.

For a short time, sleep gave me relief from my thoughts. But then, I was woken by the sound of laughter. A beautiful child had run into the area where I was hiding. He was full of joy, playing without fear. As I watched him, a thought struck me—this child was too young to know hatred. He had not yet learned to judge others by their appearance. If I could take him with me, teach him to be my companion, he could be my friend. I wouldn't have to be alone anymore.

Driven by a sudden impulse, I grabbed the boy as he ran past and pulled him toward me. The moment he saw my face, he covered his eyes and let out a piercing scream. I pulled his hands away and said, "Child, why are you screaming? I won't hurt you. Just listen to me."

He struggled with all his strength. "Let me go!" he shouted. "Monster! Ugly creature! You want to eat me, to tear me apart! You're an ogre! Let me go, or I'll tell my father!"

"You will never see your father again," I told him. "You must come with me."

"Hideous beast! Let me go! My father is an important man—he is Monsieur Frankenstein—he will punish you! You can't keep me!"

At the mention of that name, I froze. "Frankenstein! So you belong to my enemy—the one I have sworn to destroy." My voice darkened. "Then you will be my first victim."

The boy continued to fight against me, screaming insults that stabbed at my heart. I grabbed his throat to silence him, and in an instant, he lay lifeless at my feet.

I looked down at the child, and a dark satisfaction filled me. A twisted joy spread through my body as I clapped my hands and declared, "Now I too can bring misery! My enemy is not untouchable. His suffering has only begun, and I will make sure he feels pain far worse than this."

As I stared at the boy, I noticed something shining on his chest. I reached for it and discovered a small portrait of a beautiful woman. Despite my rage, I felt strangely drawn to her. Her deep, dark eyes framed by long lashes, her soft lips—her beauty captivated me. For a moment, I forgot my anger. But then the rage returned, stronger than before. I realized that I could never have the happiness that such a woman could bring. If she saw me, she would only recoil in horror and disgust.

Can you blame me for being consumed by fury? I'm only surprised that, in that moment, I didn't unleash my anger upon the whole world, destroying everything in my path.

Overcome with emotion, I left the place where I had killed the boy and searched for a more hidden spot. I came across a barn that seemed empty and entered. Inside, a young woman was sleeping on a pile of straw. She was not as breathtaking as the woman in the portrait, but she had a gentle, healthy glow. I thought bitterly, Here is yet another person who can smile and bring happiness to others—but never to me.

I leaned closer and whispered, "Wake up, my love. I am near—the one who would give everything just to see kindness in your eyes. My beloved, wake up."

She stirred slightly, and a shiver of fear ran through me. What if she woke up, saw me, and screamed? What if she cursed me and called me a murderer? She would surely do so the moment she opened her eyes and looked upon my face. The thought drove me to madness. If I had been robbed of the joy she could give, then she would suffer instead. My crime was born from my suffering—let her pay the price for it!

Thanks to Felix and the cruel laws of men, I had learned how to cause pain. I bent over her and tucked the portrait securely into the folds of her clothing. She moved again, and I fled.

For days, I remained near the place where these terrible events had happened. Sometimes, I wanted to see you. Other times, I wanted to leave this world and its misery forever. Eventually, I wandered into these mountains, where I have roamed ever since, burning with a need that only you can fulfill.

We will not part until you agree to my request. I am alone and miserable. No human will accept me. But if there were another like me—someone just as deformed, just as wretched—she would not turn away from me. I need a companion of my own kind, one who shares my suffering. You must create her.

Chapter 17

The creature finished speaking and stared at me, waiting for my response. But I was confused and overwhelmed, struggling to make sense of everything he had said. He continued,

"You must create a female like me—someone who can be my companion and share in the emotions I need to survive. Only you can do this, and I demand it as my right. You cannot refuse me."

As he spoke, my anger, which had faded while he told me about his time with the cottagers, flared up again. I could no longer hold it back.

"I refuse!" I shouted. "No amount of suffering will ever make me agree to this. You may make my life miserable, but I will never be ashamed of my own actions. Do you really think I would create another being like you—another monster that could bring more destruction to the world? Leave now! I've given you my answer. You may try to hurt me, but I will never give in."

"You are wrong," the creature replied. "I am not here to threaten you—I am here to reason with you. I am cruel because I am miserable. Everyone fears and hates me, including you, my own creator. If even you would destroy me without hesitation, then why should I care about humans? If people treated me with kindness, I would return their kindness a hundred times over. But they never will—their fear and disgust make it impossible. Still, I refuse to be a slave to their hatred. If I cannot inspire love, then I will create fear. And you, my creator, will be my greatest enemy. I swear to destroy you and make you suffer so much that you will regret ever being born."

As he spoke, his face twisted into a terrifying expression of rage, but he quickly calmed himself and continued,

"I wanted to reason with you, but my emotions get the best of me, and that is your fault. If even one being could care for me, I would dedicate my life to them. But I am left to dream of happiness that I will never have. I am only asking for something small and reasonable—a companion as hideous as I am. It may not seem like much to you, but it is all I can hope for. Yes, we will be outcasts, but that will only make us closer to each other. We may not have joyful lives, but at least we will be free from the misery I feel now. Oh, my creator, please—grant me this one request. Let me know what it feels like to be cared for, even just a little."

I hesitated. His words affected me, and I felt torn. I was horrified at what could happen if I agreed, but I also felt that his request was not completely unfair. He had emotions, he could feel pain, and as his creator, did I not owe him at least a small chance at happiness? He noticed my hesitation and pressed on.

"If you agree, neither I nor my companion will ever be seen by humans again. We will go far away to the wilds of South America, where no one will ever find us. I don't need human food—I don't harm animals. Acorns and berries are enough for me, and my companion will live the same way. We will sleep on the ground beneath the trees. The sun will shine on us just as it does on mankind, ripening the food we need. I ask for so little, and you must see that denying me would be nothing but cruel. You have been heartless toward me before, but now I see compassion in your eyes. Please—let me use this moment to convince you."

"You say you will leave mankind behind," I replied, "but how can you, who crave love and kindness, really stay in exile forever? You will return one day, searching for the companionship of humans. But when they reject you again, you will become hateful once more, and then you will have an ally to help you bring destruction. I cannot allow that to happen. Stop trying to persuade me—I cannot do this."

"How quickly your feelings change!" he said. "Just a moment ago, you seemed to understand me, and now you have hardened your heart against me again. I swear to you, on the very earth I walk upon, and on you, my creator, that if you give me a companion, I will disappear from human society forever. My anger will fade, for I will no longer be alone. My life will pass peacefully, and when I die, I will not curse the one who made me."

His words had a strange effect on me. I felt sorry for him and, at times, even wanted to comfort him. But whenever I looked at him— at the monstrous thing I had created—I was filled with horror and disgust. I tried to push these feelings aside. If I could not bring myself to love him, did I really have the right to deny him the only happiness he could ever have?

"You swear that you will live in peace," I said, "but how can I trust you? You have already shown cruelty. Should I really believe that this is not just another trick, a way for you to take your revenge on me later?"

"Why are you hesitating? I won't be ignored—I demand an answer. If I have no love and no connections, then hatred and wrongdoing will be my fate. But if I have a companion, someone to share my life with, the reason for my crimes will disappear, and I will become something no one will ever have to think about again. My cruelty comes from the loneliness that I despise, and my kindness will grow when I have someone by my side. I will finally know what it means to care for another and feel like I belong in the world instead of being shut out from it."

I sat in silence for a long time, thinking about everything he had said. I remembered how he had once shown the ability to be good, but over time, that kindness had been destroyed by rejection and hatred. I also could not ignore his strength and the danger he posed—a creature who could survive among the icy mountains and escape into unreachable places had abilities far beyond any human. After much thought, I realized that both justice for him and my responsibility to others meant that I had no choice but to agree to his request. So, I turned to him and said,

"I will do what you ask, but only if you swear to leave Europe forever, along with every place where humans live, as soon as I give you a companion to share your exile."

"I swear it!" he cried. "I swear by the sun, the sky, and by the fire of longing in my heart. If you grant my request, you will never see me again as long as I live. Now go home and begin your work. I will watch from afar, waiting with unbearable anticipation. Do not fear—I will come when the time is right."

With that, he suddenly left, perhaps afraid that I might change my mind. I watched as he rushed down the mountain with the speed of an eagle, disappearing among the icy ridges.

His story had lasted the entire day, and as he left, the sun was setting. I knew I needed to hurry down the mountain before darkness surrounded me, but my heart was heavy, and I walked slowly. My thoughts were tangled, and the effort of carefully stepping along the winding, narrow paths only added to my exhaustion. By the time I reached the halfway resting spot, night had fully set in. I sat beside a fountain, staring at the sky. The stars flickered between passing clouds, the dark pine trees stood tall, and fallen branches lay scattered around me. It was a quiet and eerie scene, filling my mind with strange thoughts. Overwhelmed, I buried my face in my hands and sobbed. Then, looking up, I cried out, "Oh, stars, clouds, and winds, do you mock me too? If you feel any pity, take away my thoughts and memories—let me disappear. But if you won't, then leave me alone in the dark."

My mind was wild with misery, and I can't explain how the endless twinkling of the stars seemed to press down on me or how the sound of the wind filled me with dread, as if it carried some unseen doom toward me.

Morning had already arrived by the time I reached the village of Chamounix. I did not rest but continued my journey straight back to Geneva. I could not put my feelings into words—they weighed on me like a crushing burden, so heavy that they dulled even my pain. When I finally arrived home, I walked inside and faced my family. My appearance—wild and exhausted—alarmed them, but I did not answer their questions. I could barely speak. I felt as if I were cursed, as if I had lost the right to be close to them, as if I would never again be part of their lives. And yet, despite this, I loved them more than anything. To protect them, I would force myself to complete the most horrible task of my life. The thought of creating another creature like him filled me with dread, but it was the only thing that felt real to me now—everything else in my life seemed distant, like a dream.

Chapter 18

Day after day, week after week, went by as I traveled back to Geneva, but I still couldn't bring myself to start my work again. I was afraid of what the monster might do if I failed him, yet the thought of creating another being like him filled me with dread. I knew that making a female creature would take months of hard work and careful study. I had heard about an English scientist who had made important discoveries that could help me, and sometimes I thought about asking my father for permission to go to England. But I kept finding reasons to delay my work, convincing myself that it wasn't as urgent as I had first believed.

During this time, I noticed a change in myself. My health, which had been steadily declining, had improved, and my spirits lifted when I wasn't thinking about my dreadful promise. My father was pleased to see me looking better, but he still worried about the moments when sadness overtook me. At those times, I would isolate myself completely. I spent entire days alone on the lake in a small boat, staring at the sky and listening to the gentle sounds of the water. I was silent and lost in thought. But the fresh air and sunshine often calmed me, and when I returned home, I was able to greet my family with a more natural smile.

One evening, after coming back from one of these quiet outings, my father pulled me aside to speak to me privately.

"My dear son, I am happy to see you returning to the things you once enjoyed. You seem more like yourself again. But I can tell that something is still troubling you. You keep avoiding us, and I have spent a long time trying to understand why. Yesterday, a thought occurred to me, and if I am right, I beg you to tell me the truth. Hiding your feelings will only bring more pain to all of us."

I felt a shiver of fear as he spoke, but he continued.

"I must confess that I have always expected you and Elizabeth to marry. I have believed that your union would bring happiness to our family and give me peace in my old age. You two grew up together, studied side by side, and seemed to share the same interests and values. But perhaps I was wrong. Maybe you see her only as a sister and do not wish to make her your wife. Or perhaps you love another, but feel bound to Elizabeth out of duty, causing you great inner turmoil. If that is the case, you must tell me."

"My dear father," I replied, "you can put your worries to rest. I love Elizabeth deeply and truly. No other woman has ever inspired the love and admiration that I feel for her. My future and my happiness are tied to the hope of our marriage."

His face brightened at my words. "Hearing this brings me more joy than I have felt in a long time. If you feel this way, then despite our recent hardships, we can still look forward to happiness. But I see that your mind is troubled, and I want to ease that burden. So tell me—do you object to marrying Elizabeth soon? We have suffered misfortune, and life has not been as peaceful as I would wish, but you are young. You already have a comfortable fortune, and an early marriage would not interfere with any future plans you may have. However, I do not wish to pressure you. If you want to wait, I will not be upset. I only ask you to be honest with me."

I stood in silence, unable to answer right away. My thoughts raced in every direction as I tried to make sense of what I should do. The idea of marrying Elizabeth should have filled me with joy, yet instead, I felt horror and despair. I was still bound by a promise I had not yet fulfilled, and I could not risk breaking it. If I refused the monster, what terrible fate might he bring upon me and my family? How could I celebrate a wedding with the weight of this terrifying duty crushing me? I had to complete my work and ensure the monster left with his companion before I could allow myself to find peace.

I also realized that I had another obstacle—whether I should travel to England or spend months writing letters to the scientists there. The second option would be slow and uncertain. More importantly, I could not bear the thought of working on my horrifying task while living under my father's roof, surrounded by the people I loved. If I stayed, there was too much risk that something would go wrong—that they would discover my work and be horrified by the truth. I also knew that the stress and disgust I would feel while creating the creature would make it impossible to hide my emotions. I would have to go somewhere far away, where I could be completely alone. Once I began, I hoped I could finish quickly and return to my family in peace. Maybe, I foolishly imagined, something might even happen to the monster before then, freeing me from my duty forever.

With these thoughts in mind, I answered my father. I told him I wished to visit England but kept my real reasons a secret. Instead, I made my request sound natural and reasonable so that he would not suspect anything. Seeing that I had been lost in sorrow for so long, my father was relieved to hear that I wanted to travel. He hoped that a change of scenery and new experiences would help restore my spirits. Little did he know the real purpose of my journey.

The length of my journey was left up to me. It could last a few months or even a year at most. My father, wanting to ensure I had company, had secretly arranged with Elizabeth for Clerval to meet me in Strasburgh. At first, I disliked the idea since I wanted to be alone to focus on my work. But in the beginning, having my friend with me wouldn't be a problem. In fact, I was relieved that I wouldn't have to spend all my time lost in my dark thoughts. Besides, Clerval's presence might even keep the monster from appearing and reminding me of my dreadful task.

I was bound for England, and it was understood that once I returned, I would marry Elizabeth. My father, growing older, didn't want to delay the wedding. For me, there was only one thing that gave me comfort as I prepared for this terrible task—the hope that once it was finished, I could finally be free. I imagined the day when I could return home, claim Elizabeth as my wife, and leave my nightmares behind.

As I prepared to leave, I couldn't shake the fear that my loved ones would be left defenseless against the monster. What if, in his anger, he decided to harm them while I was gone? But then I reminded myself that he had sworn to follow me wherever I went. That thought was terrifying, but at least it meant my family would be safe. Still, I couldn't be sure. I had no choice but to trust that the creature would keep his word.

At the end of September, I left my homeland once again. The journey was my own idea, and Elizabeth, though she agreed, was worried about me. She feared that being away from home would only bring me more suffering. Wanting to make sure I had a companion, she had arranged for Clerval to join me. Women often notice details that men overlook, and she had seen how much I needed a friend. As she said goodbye, she struggled to speak, her emotions overwhelming her.

I climbed into the carriage, barely aware of where I was going. My thoughts were dark and heavy. The only thing I remembered to do was to order my chemical instruments to be packed and sent with me. As I traveled through breathtaking landscapes, I barely noticed them. My mind was consumed by the task ahead.

After days of aimless travel, I reached Strasburgh and waited two days for Clerval to arrive. When he finally did, the difference between us was striking. He was full of energy and excitement, thrilled by every new sight. He marveled at the sunset and the beauty of the world around us. "This is what it means to truly live!" he exclaimed. "I feel so alive! But you, my dear Frankenstein, why are you so sad?" I barely heard him. My mind was filled with dark thoughts. I didn't notice the stars appearing in the evening sky or the golden light of the sunrise. If you had read Clerval's travel journal, you would have found joy in his descriptions. But my thoughts were filled only with misery and the curse that followed me.

We had planned to travel down the Rhine by boat from Strasburgh to Rotterdam, where we would then set sail for London. Along the way, we passed through islands lined with willow trees and saw many charming towns. We stopped in Mannheim for a day, and on the fifth day of our journey, we reached Mainz. From there, the Rhine became even more beautiful. The river flowed swiftly through steep, rolling hills. We saw ruined castles standing on the edges of cliffs, surrounded by dark forests. In one moment, we would see jagged rocks and a rushing river beneath us, and in the next, the scenery would change to green vineyards and peaceful villages.

It was the time of the grape harvest, and we heard the songs of the workers as we drifted down the river. Even in my sorrow, I couldn't help but feel some sense of peace. Lying at the bottom of the boat, staring up at the clear blue sky, I felt a kind of calm that I hadn't known in a long time. If I, with all my grief, could feel even a moment of tranquility, then you can imagine the happiness Clerval felt. To him, it was like stepping into a dream.

"I have seen the most beautiful places in my own country," Clerval said. "I have visited the lakes of Lucerne and Uri, where the towering mountains cast dark shadows over the water. I have seen the violent storms that shake the lakes, making the waves crash against the cliffs where legends say lost lovers still cry out in the wind. I have seen the mighty peaks of La Valais and the Pays de Vaud. But this river, Victor, is more beautiful than all of them. The mountains of Switzerland are grand and wild, but the Rhine has a charm that I have never seen before. Look at that castle clinging to the cliffside, and the one on the island, hidden among the trees. And there—see the workers coming in from the vineyards? Look at that village tucked into the mountainside. Surely, the spirit that watches over this place is kinder to mankind than the ones that rule over our frozen peaks."

Clerval! My dear friend! Even now, I find comfort in remembering your words and thinking about the kindness and brilliance that made you so special. You seemed to be created from the very essence of nature's beauty. Your imagination was wild and full of wonder, but it was balanced by the kindness in your heart. You were filled with deep emotions, and your friendship was so strong and pure that it seemed like something out of a story, something too rare for the real world. But even the love and companionship of others were not enough for your restless mind. While most people admired nature from a distance, you truly loved it.

The roaring waterfalls
Filled him with longing; the towering cliffs,
The mountains, and the shadowy forests—
Their colors and shapes stirred something deep inside him,
A craving, a feeling, and a love
That needed no explanation,
No hidden meaning, no added beauty,
Only what his eyes could behold.

And where is he now? Is this kind, wonderful person truly gone forever? Can a mind so full of ideas and dreams—so capable of creating an entire world within itself—simply vanish? No, I cannot believe that. His beautiful form may have faded, but his spirit still lingers, bringing comfort to his heartbroken friend.

Forgive my sorrow. These words feel like such a small tribute to Henry, who was so extraordinary, but they ease my pain, even just a little. I will continue my story.

After passing through Cologne, we entered the flatlands of Holland. The scenery was no longer as breathtaking as before, and since the wind was against us and the river's current was too weak to help us along, we decided to travel the rest of the way by carriage. A few days later, we reached Rotterdam, where we boarded a ship for England.

It was a clear morning in late December when I first caught sight of the white cliffs of Britain. As we sailed along the Thames, a new landscape unfolded before us. The land was flat but rich and fertile, with towns scattered along the river, each carrying a story from history. We passed Tilbury Fort, reminding us of the Spanish Armada, then saw Gravesend, Woolwich, and Greenwich—places I had heard of even from my home country.

At last, the many church steeples of London came into view, with St. Paul's Cathedral standing tall above them all, and the Tower of London—a place so deeply woven into English history—looming in the distance.

Chapter 19

London was our planned resting place, and we decided to stay there for several months. Clerval was eager to meet the great thinkers and talented individuals of the time, but for me, that was less important. My main focus was gathering the knowledge I needed to complete my promise, so I quickly used the letters of introduction I had brought to meet the most respected scientists.

If I had taken this journey during my days of happiness and learning, I would have found great joy in it. But now, my life felt cursed, and I only visited these people for the information they could provide. I found no comfort in company; instead, I preferred to be alone, where I could distract myself by observing the sky and land around me. Clerval's voice sometimes soothed me, helping me find brief moments of peace. However, seeing busy, cheerful faces reminded me of my misery. I felt as if a wall had been built between me and the rest of the world, a wall stained with the blood of William and Justine. Thinking about them filled me with sorrow.

Clerval, on the other hand, was full of curiosity and eager to learn. He found joy in observing different customs and ways of life. He also had a goal—he wanted to visit India. He believed that his knowledge of its languages and culture would help advance trade and European influence there. England was the best place for him to continue his preparations. He was always occupied with his plans, and the only thing that troubled him was my sadness. I tried to hide my feelings so that I wouldn't take away from his excitement. Sometimes, I made excuses to avoid joining him, preferring to be alone. At the same time, I began gathering the materials I needed for my terrible work. Every step of the process felt like torture, as if drops of water were constantly falling onto my head. Thinking about it brought me pain, and even mentioning it made me tremble.

After spending several months in London, we received a letter from a man in Scotland who had once visited us in Geneva. He described the beauty of his homeland and invited us to visit him in Perth. Clerval was eager to go, and although I hated socializing, I longed to see mountains, rivers, and the wonders of nature once more.

We had arrived in England in early October, and it was now February. We decided to begin our journey north in about a month. Instead of taking the main road to Edinburgh, we planned to travel through Windsor, Oxford, Matlock, and the lakes of Cumberland, expecting to complete our trip by the end of July. I packed my scientific tools and materials, planning to finish my dreadful task in some remote part of the Scottish Highlands.

On March 27th, we left London and spent a few days in Windsor, wandering through its beautiful forests. As mountain dwellers, this was a new experience for us. The towering oak trees, large numbers of wild animals, and herds of majestic deer were unfamiliar sights.

Next, we traveled to Oxford. As we entered the city, we thought about the events that had taken place there over 150 years earlier. This was where King Charles I had gathered his forces, and even after the rest of the country turned against him to support Parliament and freedom, the city had remained loyal. Remembering the king's tragic fate, along with figures like the noble Falkland, the arrogant Goring, and the queen and prince, made every part of the city feel significant. It felt as though history still lived in its streets, and we enjoyed imagining the past within its walls. Even without these reflections, Oxford was a place of beauty. Its ancient colleges were charming, its streets grand, and the serene river Isis flowed beside the city, reflecting its towers, spires, and domes, all surrounded by lush green meadows and old trees.

I admired the scenery around me, but my enjoyment was clouded by memories of the past and fears for the future. I had been created for a life of peace and happiness. As a child, I had never been troubled by deep sadness, and if I ever felt bored, the beauty of nature or the brilliance of human creativity could always lift my spirits. But now, I felt like a tree that had been struck by lightning—my soul was wounded, and I believed I would live only to become a miserable reminder of what I had lost, pitied by others but unbearable to myself.

We spent a long time in Oxford, wandering through its surroundings and searching for places connected to important moments in English history. Our curiosity often led us to extend our explorations, drawn in by new discoveries at every turn. We visited the grave of the great patriot Hampden and the battlefield where he had died. For a moment, my mind was lifted above my own suffering as I thought about the noble ideals of freedom and self-sacrifice that these places represented. I dared to imagine myself free of my burdens, but my pain quickly returned, pulling me back into despair.

With reluctance, we left Oxford and traveled to Matlock, our next stop. The landscape there reminded me of Switzerland, though on a smaller scale. The green hills lacked the towering white Alps that surrounded my homeland's pine-covered mountains. We explored the famous cave and the small natural history collections, which were arranged like the displays in Servoz and Chamonix. Hearing Henry mention Chamonix made me shudder, as it brought back terrible memories, and I was eager to leave Matlock behind.

From Derby, we continued north, spending two months in Cumberland and Westmorland. The scenery reminded me even more of the Swiss mountains. The patches of snow still clinging to the northern slopes, the lakes, and the rushing streams among the rocks all felt familiar and comforting. During our stay, we met new acquaintances who almost made me forget my troubles for a short time. Clerval was even happier than I was. Surrounded by talented and intelligent people, he felt inspired and discovered new strengths in himself that he hadn't realized before. "I could live here forever," he told me. "Among these mountains, I would hardly miss Switzerland or the Rhine."

But he soon learned that traveling was not all pleasure—it also brought its share of hardship. Just as he began to settle into one place and enjoy it, he had to leave and move on to the next. He constantly found new wonders, but before long, he was forced to say goodbye to them.

We had barely finished exploring the beautiful lakes of Cumberland and Westmorland and had just begun forming attachments to some of the people there when it was time to continue our journey to meet our Scottish friend. I didn't mind leaving. I had been putting off my promise for too long, and I feared how the monster might react to my delay. He might still be in Switzerland, seeking revenge on my family. This thought haunted me, ruining any chance I had for peace. I anxiously waited for letters from home, and if they were late, I was filled with terrible fear. When they arrived, and I saw Elizabeth's or my father's handwriting, I could barely bring myself to open them, afraid of what news they might bring. At times, I even imagined that the monster was following me, waiting for an opportunity to punish me by harming my friend. When these dark thoughts consumed me, I refused to leave Henry's side, determined to protect him. It felt as though I had committed a terrible crime, and the guilt of it weighed heavily on me. Though I was innocent, I had still brought a terrible curse upon myself—one just as heavy as if I had done something truly wicked.

I visited Edinburgh with little interest, though it was a city that could have fascinated anyone. Clerval didn't like it as much as Oxford, which he found more charming because of its ancient buildings. But the beauty and order of Edinburgh's newer areas, its dramatic castle, and its stunning surroundings, including Arthur's Seat, St. Bernard's Well, and the Pentland Hills, helped make up for it. He admired them all with excitement, but I was impatient to reach my final destination.

After a week, we left Edinburgh, passing through Coupar and St. Andrews before following the Tay River to Perth, where our friend was waiting for us. But I was in no mood to socialize, to laugh with strangers, or to engage in polite conversation as a guest was expected to. So, I told Clerval that I wanted to continue traveling alone.

"Go and enjoy yourself," I said. "Let's agree on a meeting place, and I will return in a month or two. But please, don't ask questions or try to change my mind. I need some time alone. When I come back, I hope my heart will be lighter and more in tune with your cheerful nature."

Henry tried to convince me otherwise, but when he saw that I was determined, he gave up. Instead, he asked me to write to him often. "I would rather travel with you," he admitted. "I don't know these Scottish people, and I won't feel at home without you. So, return soon, my dear friend."

After leaving my friend, I decided to find a remote place in Scotland where I could work alone. I had no doubt that the monster was following me and would appear when I finished, ready to claim his companion.

With this plan in mind, I traveled through the northern highlands and chose one of the farthest Orkney Islands as my workplace. It was the perfect place for such a task—just a barren rock constantly battered by the waves. The land was poor, barely providing enough grass for a few thin cows and enough oats to feed the few people who lived there. Only five people called this island home, and their thin, frail bodies showed how little they had to eat. Even basic supplies like vegetables, bread, and fresh water had to be brought in from the mainland, which was five miles away.

There were only three small huts on the entire island, and one of them was empty when I arrived. I rented it. The hut had just two rooms, both in terrible condition. The thatched roof was falling apart, the walls were bare, and the door barely hung on its hinges. I had the place fixed up, bought some basic furniture, and moved in. Normally, a stranger settling in such an isolated place would have been cause for curiosity, but the islanders were too worn down by poverty and hardship to care. They barely noticed me, not even offering thanks when I gave them food or clothing. It seemed their suffering had dulled even the simplest human emotions.

Each morning, I focused on my work, but in the evenings, when the weather allowed, I walked along the rocky shore, listening to the waves crash against the land. The sea was both repetitive and ever-changing. I thought of Switzerland—so different from this bleak and lonely place. Its hills were covered in vineyards, cottages dotted the landscape, and its lakes reflected a bright, gentle sky. Even when stirred by the wind, the waters of Switzerland were calm compared to the fierce, raging ocean around me.

At first, I followed this routine, but as my work progressed, it became more unbearable every day. Some days, I couldn't bring myself to enter my workshop at all. Other times, I forced myself to work day and night, desperate to finish as quickly as possible. The process was disgusting. The first time I had done this, I had been so caught up in the excitement of creation that I ignored the horror of what I was doing. My mind had been completely focused on my goal, and I had shut out everything else. But now, I worked with full awareness of my actions, and it made me sick.

Alone with my dreadful task, I became restless and anxious. I constantly feared that the monster would appear at any moment. Sometimes, I sat staring at the ground, afraid to lift my eyes in case I saw him standing there. I even hesitated to leave my hut, worried that if I were alone, he would come to claim what he had been promised.

Despite my fear, I continued working, and I had made a great deal of progress. I looked forward to finishing with both eagerness and dread. I didn't let myself question the hope I felt, but deep down, a sense of unease weighed on me. Something felt wrong, and the thought of what might happen next made my heart sink.

Chapter 20

One evening, I sat in my workshop. The sun had set, and the moon had just begun to rise over the sea. The light was too dim for me to continue working, so I paused, unsure whether to stop for the night or push forward to finish my task. As I sat there, deep in thought, I began to consider the consequences of what I was about to do.

Three years earlier, I had created a monster, and his cruelty had filled my life with misery and regret. Now, I was about to bring another creature into existence, but I knew nothing about what she would be like. She could be even more dangerous than the first, taking pleasure in destruction and suffering. He had sworn to leave human society and live in the wilderness, but she had not made that promise. She would have a mind of her own and might refuse to follow his plan. What if they didn't even like each other? He already hated his own appearance—would he despise it even more when he saw it in another being? And what if she rejected him, turning instead to humans, drawn to their beauty? If she left him, his anger and loneliness might grow even stronger.

Even if they stayed together and fled to distant lands, their bond could lead to something far worse—the creation of a new race of monsters. Their children could spread across the earth, threatening humanity itself. Did I have the right to bring such a curse upon future generations, just to free myself from my own suffering? Before, I had been swayed by the monster's arguments and frightened by his threats. But now, for the first time, I saw the full horror of what I was about to do. If I went through with this, future generations might curse me for dooming the human race, all because I had been too selfish to say no.

I shuddered, and my heart pounded in fear. Then, as I looked up, I saw the monster standing at the window, his face twisted into a terrible grin. He had followed me all this time, hiding in forests, caves, and empty fields, waiting for me to fulfill my promise. Now, he had come to see my progress and claim his reward.

As I stared at him, I saw nothing but malice and deceit in his expression. Overwhelmed with horror, I thought about what I was doing. My hands trembled with rage, and in a sudden burst of anger, I ripped apart the half-finished creature before me. The monster watched in shock as I destroyed the one thing he had been waiting for. With a howl of fury and despair, he turned and disappeared into the night.

Shaking, I locked the door behind me and swore to myself that I would never continue this terrible work. Then, unsteady on my feet, I returned to my own room, where I sat alone, trapped in my own dark thoughts.

Hours passed as I stared out at the sea. The water was still, the wind silent, and everything lay under the soft glow of the moon. Now and then, I could hear fishermen calling to each other from their boats in the distance. I barely noticed the deep quiet around me until the sound of oars suddenly broke the silence. Someone was rowing toward the shore. A few minutes later, I heard the faint creak of my door as if someone was trying to open it quietly.

Terror gripped me. I knew who it must be. I wanted to call for help from a nearby cottage, but my fear paralyzed me, just like in a nightmare when you try to run but cannot move. I stood frozen, unable to act.

Then I heard slow footsteps coming down the hall. The door swung open, and there he was—the monster I had been dreading. He shut the door behind him and walked toward me. His voice was low and threatening as he spoke.

"You have destroyed what you began. What are you planning to do now? Do you dare to break your promise? I have suffered and struggled—I left Switzerland and followed you along the Rhine, through the fields of England, and across the wilds of Scotland. I have endured hunger, cold, and exhaustion. And now you dare to take away my only hope?"

"Go away!" I shouted. "I will not keep my promise. I will never create another creature like you, another being as twisted and evil."

The monster's eyes darkened. "I tried to reason with you before, but you have proven yourself unworthy of my patience. Remember this—I have power. You think you are miserable now, but I can make you suffer so much that you will curse the daylight. You may have created me, but I am your master now. Obey me!"

I met his glare and stood firm. "I have made my decision, and your threats will not change it. I will not bring another monster into this world. How could I, in cold blood, unleash another creature who finds joy in death and suffering? Leave now—I will not do it, and your words will only make me more certain."

The monster saw the determination on my face and ground his teeth in frustration. "So every man may have a wife, and every creature a mate—but I must remain alone?" he growled. "I have longed for love and companionship, but instead, I have been met only with disgust and hatred. Fine! Hate me if you must, but be warned—your life will be filled with fear and suffering. I will take away everything you hold dear. Do you think you can be happy while I live in misery? No! You can destroy my dreams, but you cannot take away my revenge. I will make you pay for all you have done to me. I may die, but before that happens, you will curse the very sun that shines upon your pain. Beware, Frankenstein—I have nothing to lose, and that makes me powerful. I will wait, like a snake in the grass, until the perfect moment comes. You will regret the pain you have caused me."

"Stop, monster! Don't fill the air with your hateful words. I have made my decision, and I am not weak enough to change my mind because of threats. Leave me; nothing will make me change my mind."

"Very well," he replied. "I will go, but remember—I will be there on your wedding night."

I jumped up and shouted, "You villain! Before you threaten my life, make sure your own is safe!"

I tried to grab him, but he was too quick. He rushed out of the house, and within moments, I saw him in his boat, gliding swiftly across the water until he disappeared into the waves.

Silence filled the air once more, but his words echoed in my mind. I was burning with anger, desperate to chase him down and throw him into the sea. I paced back and forth in my room, my mind racing with terrible thoughts. Why had I let him go? Why hadn't I fought him then and there? Now he was heading toward the mainland, and I shuddered to think who his next victim might be.

Then, his words rang in my head again—"I will be with you on your wedding night." So that was when he planned to strike. He intended to kill me, and that would be the moment when his revenge was complete. The thought didn't scare me, but when I imagined Elizabeth—her tears, her endless grief when she found her husband cruelly taken from her—I broke down. For the first time in months, I wept. I vowed that I would not fall to my enemy without a fight.

The night passed, and the sun rose over the ocean. My rage had faded, replaced by a deep, hollow despair. I left the house, walking along the shore, staring at the vast sea as if it were a wall separating me from the rest of the world. A strange thought crossed my mind—maybe it would be better if I stayed here forever, living in lonely misery but free from sudden shocks of suffering. If I returned home, I knew I would either be killed or watch the people I loved fall victim to the monster I had created.

I wandered the island like a restless ghost, cut off from everything and everyone I loved. When the sun was high in the sky, exhaustion finally overtook me. I lay down on the grass and fell into a deep sleep. I had been awake all night, my nerves frayed, my eyes sore from sleeplessness and misery. That sleep refreshed me, and when I woke, I felt more connected to the world again. But the creature's words still echoed in my mind, haunting me like a nightmare that refused to fade.

The sun had nearly set when I sat on the shore, eating a simple oatcake to satisfy my hunger. Just then, I noticed a small fishing boat landing nearby. A man stepped out and handed me a packet of letters. Inside, I found letters from Geneva—and one from Clerval, urging me to join him. He wrote that he was wasting time where he was and had received letters from his friends in London calling him back to complete an important business deal for his journey to India. He couldn't delay much longer, but since he might leave for his voyage soon, he begged me to spend as much time with him as I could before he left. He asked me to leave my lonely island and meet him in Perth so we could travel south together.

His letter brought me back to reality, and I decided I would leave in two days. But before I could go, there was something I had to do—something that made my skin crawl just thinking about it. I needed to pack up my chemical instruments, which meant I had to step back into the room where I had worked on my terrible creation. I had to touch the tools that now filled me with disgust.

At dawn the next day, I gathered the courage to unlock the laboratory door. Inside, the remains of the half-formed creature I had destroyed were scattered across the floor. For a moment, I felt like I had torn apart a real human body. I hesitated, then forced myself to enter. My hands shook as I carried the instruments out, but I knew I couldn't leave behind any trace of my work. The villagers might see the remains and be horrified. I placed them in a basket, weighing it down with heavy stones, planning to throw it into the sea that night. Until then, I sat on the beach, cleaning and organizing my equipment.

My feelings had completely changed since the night the monster appeared. Before, I had seen my promise as a horrible duty that I had no choice but to fulfill. But now, it was as if a veil had been lifted from my eyes—I finally saw the truth. The idea of continuing my work never even crossed my mind. His threats still hung over me, but I never once considered that I could escape them by giving in to his demands. I knew deep down that creating another monster would be an act of selfishness and cruelty. I would never allow myself to think otherwise.

Around two or three in the morning, the moon rose. I carried my basket to a small boat and sailed about four miles from shore. The sea was empty except for a few fishing boats heading back to land, but I steered away from them. It felt as if I were committing some terrible crime, and I avoided people as though I feared being caught. As I reached the right spot, the moon, once bright, suddenly disappeared behind a thick cloud. Seizing the moment of darkness, I dropped the basket into the water. I listened as it sank, the sound gurgling through the still night. Then, I turned my boat and rowed away from the spot.

The sky grew cloudy, and a cool breeze from the northeast began to rise. Though the air was cold, it refreshed me, filling me with a strange sense of relief. I decided to stay out on the water a little longer. Setting the rudder to keep the boat steady, I lay down at the bottom. Darkness surrounded me, the moon hidden behind thick clouds. The only sound was the gentle murmur of the waves against the boat. That soft, steady rhythm calmed me, and before long, I drifted into a deep sleep.

I had no idea how long I had been asleep, but when I woke up, the sun was already high in the sky. The wind was strong, and the waves crashed against my small boat, threatening to overturn it. I quickly realized that the wind had pushed me far from the coast where I had started. I tried to change direction, but as soon as I attempted it, the boat nearly filled with water. Seeing no other choice, I let the wind carry me further out to sea.

Fear crept into my heart. I had no compass, and I barely knew the geography of this area. The sun was little help in guiding me. I could be drifting toward the vast Atlantic, where I might starve or be swallowed by the endless waves that surrounded me. I had already been at sea for hours, and a terrible thirst burned in my throat—a warning of the suffering still to come. I looked up at the sky, covered in fast-moving clouds, one after another racing across the heavens. I looked down at the sea, realizing that this could be my grave. "Monster," I cried, "you have already won!"

My mind filled with thoughts of Elizabeth, my father, and Clerval—those I had left behind, vulnerable to the monster's fury. The thought of them suffering at his hands sent me into a deep despair, so painful that even now, as I recall it, I shudder.

Hours passed. The sun moved lower in the sky, and slowly, the wind began to calm. The waves that had threatened to swallow me turned into a steady rolling motion that made me feel sick and weak. Just as I was about to give in to exhaustion, I saw a dark line of land in the distance.

A rush of hope flooded through me. For hours, I had feared that I was doomed, but now, I knew I would live. Tears filled my eyes. It's strange how, even in the worst suffering, we still cling to life. Using part of my clothing, I made another sail and guided the boat toward the shore. As I got closer, I saw that the land was wild and rocky, but there were signs of farming and human life. I spotted ships near the coast and suddenly realized I was back near civilization.

Following the coastline, I eventually saw a church steeple rise behind a small stretch of land. Feeling weak, I decided to head straight for the town, knowing I could find food and rest there. Thankfully, I still had money with me. As I rounded the point, I saw a neat little town with a good harbor, and my heart leaped with relief—I had escaped death.

As I tied up the boat and adjusted the sails, a crowd gathered around me. At first, I thought they were just curious, but soon I noticed something strange. Instead of offering help, they whispered among themselves, their faces full of suspicion. Normally, this would have made me uneasy, but I was too tired to care. I simply noticed that they were speaking English and decided to ask for help.

"My friends," I said, "can you tell me the name of this town and where exactly I am?"

"You'll find out soon enough," said a rough-looking man, with a harsh voice. "You may not like this place much, but you won't have a choice about staying."

I was shocked by his rude answer and confused by the angry expressions around me. "Why are you speaking to me this way?" I asked. "Surely, Englishmen do not treat strangers so harshly."

"I don't know about English customs," the man replied coldly, "but in Ireland, we don't take kindly to villains."

As we spoke, more and more people gathered, their eyes filled with a mix of curiosity and anger. Their attitude unsettled me. I asked for directions to an inn, but no one answered. When I tried to walk away, murmurs spread through the crowd, and people closed in around me.

Then, a rough-looking man stepped forward, tapped me on the shoulder, and said, "Come with me, sir. You must speak with Mr. Kirwin and explain yourself."

"Who is Mr. Kirwin? Why do I need to explain myself? Isn't this a free country?"

"Yes, sir, free for honest men. Mr. Kirwin is the magistrate, and you need to answer for a murder that happened here last night."

His words hit me like a hammer. For a moment, I was too stunned to speak. But then I reminded myself—I was innocent. I had nothing to fear because the truth would prove me guiltless. So, without resisting, I followed the man in silence to one of the finest houses in town.

I was weak from exhaustion and hunger, barely able to stand, but I forced myself to stay strong. I didn't want my physical weakness to be mistaken for guilt or fear. At that moment, I had no idea that something far worse was about to happen—something that would make me forget all my fears of shame or even death.

I must pause here. It takes all my strength to bring back the terrible events that followed and describe them in full detail.

Chapter 21

I was soon brought before the magistrate, an elderly man with a calm and kind manner. However, he looked at me with some suspicion before turning to the men who had brought me in, asking who would testify as witnesses.

About six men stepped forward, and one of them was chosen to speak first. He explained that he had gone out fishing the night before with his son and his brother-in-law, Daniel Nugent. Around ten o'clock, they noticed strong winds coming from the north and decided to return to shore. It was a dark night since the moon had not yet risen, so instead of landing at the main harbor, they went to a small creek about two miles away. The fisherman walked ahead, carrying some of their gear, while the others followed at a short distance. As he made his way along the sand, he suddenly tripped over something and fell. When his companions reached him with their lantern, they saw that he had fallen over the body of a man.

At first, they thought the body had washed up from the sea, but when they examined it more closely, they realized that the clothes were dry and the body was still warm. They carried it to a nearby cottage and tried to revive him, but it was useless. The man was young—about twenty-five years old—and had no visible wounds except for dark marks on his neck, as if someone had strangled him.

At first, I felt nothing but mild interest in the testimony, but when they described the marks on the victim's neck, I was hit with a terrible realization. It reminded me of my brother's murder. My body trembled, and my vision blurred. I had to lean on a chair to steady myself. The magistrate noticed my reaction and looked at me closely, clearly taking it as a bad sign.

The fisherman's son then confirmed his father's story. When Daniel Nugent spoke, he swore that just before the body was found, he had seen a small boat near the shore with only one person inside. He claimed it looked like the very boat I had arrived in.

A woman who lived near the beach testified that she had been standing outside her cottage, waiting for the fishermen to return, when she saw a boat with a single man push off from the shore. This was about an hour before the body was discovered.

Another woman confirmed that the fishermen had brought the body to her house. She said it was still warm when they placed it in a bed and tried to revive him. Daniel had run into town to fetch a doctor, but by then, it was too late.

Several other men testified about my arrival. They pointed out that the strong wind during the night could have easily caused me to drift for hours and end up back near the same spot where I had started. Some even suggested that I had brought the body from elsewhere and landed in the harbor by accident, unaware of how close I was to the crime scene.

After hearing all of this, Mr. Kirwin, the magistrate, ordered me to be taken to see the body. He wanted to observe my reaction, especially since I had shown such distress when they described how the victim had been killed. With several others, I was taken to an inn where the body was being kept.

As I entered the room and approached the coffin, a terrible feeling came over me. Even now, I shudder to think about it. Everything around me—the magistrate, the witnesses, the entire situation—faded from my mind the moment I saw who it was.

Henry Clerval.

My dear friend lay lifeless before me. I gasped for air and, overcome with horror, threw myself over his body. "Have I caused your death too, Henry?" I cried out. "Two are already dead because of me, and more will soon follow. But you, Clerval—my friend, my brother in all but blood—how could this happen?"

I could take no more. My body collapsed in violent convulsions, and I was carried out of the room.

A raging fever followed, and for two months, I lay on the edge of death. I later learned that during my illness, my ravings had been terrifying. I screamed that I was the murderer of William, Justine, and Clerval. I begged my caretakers to help me destroy the monster that tormented me. Other times, I felt as though the creature's fingers were wrapped around my throat, and I screamed in agony. Only Mr. Kirwin, who spoke my language, understood what I was saying, but my wild cries and frantic gestures frightened even those who could not comprehend my words.

Why didn't I die? Why was I forced to live while others—innocent, beloved—were taken so easily? So many young, hopeful lives are cut short, leaving behind grieving families. How was I, burdened with endless misery, able to survive such suffering?

But I was not meant to die. After two months, I slowly recovered, as if waking from a terrible nightmare. When I finally became aware of my surroundings, I realized I was in a prison cell. I lay on a rough bed, surrounded by guards, locked doors, and the cold, dreary air of a dungeon.

Morning light streamed through the barred windows, and for a moment, I could not remember where I was or why I was there. I only felt an overwhelming sense of sorrow, like some terrible tragedy had befallen me. Then, as I took in my grim surroundings, the memories crashed down on me. I groaned in despair.

The sound woke an old woman who had been sitting beside me, sleeping in a chair. She was my nurse, the wife of one of the prison guards. Her face was harsh and indifferent, as if she had spent her life seeing suffering without ever feeling sympathy. When she spoke, her voice was cold and unfeeling.

"Are you feeling better, sir?" she asked.

In a weak voice, I answered, "I think so. But if all of this is real— if I am not dreaming—I almost wish I had not survived."

"If you mean what happened to the man you killed," she replied, "then yes, you might be better off dead. I expect things won't go well for you. But that's not my concern. My job is to take care of you and help you get better. I do my duty with a clear conscience. If only everyone did the same."

I turned away in disgust from the woman who could say something so heartless to someone who had just barely escaped death. But I felt weak and too tired to think about everything that had happened. My whole life felt like a dream—I even doubted if it was real because it never seemed solid in my mind.

As the memories became clearer, I started feeling feverish. A heavy darkness surrounded me. There was no one there to comfort me with a kind voice or a gentle touch. The doctor came and gave me medicine, which the old woman prepared. But he didn't seem to care, and her face was full of cruelty. Who would care about a murderer, except the executioner who would be paid to end his life?

At first, these were my thoughts. But soon, I learned that Mr. Kirwin had actually been very kind to me. He arranged for me to have the best room in the prison (though even the best was still miserable). He also provided a doctor and a nurse. He didn't visit often—not because he didn't care, but because he couldn't bear to watch the suffering of someone accused of such a terrible crime. Still, he made sure I wasn't being mistreated, though his visits were short and infrequent.

One day, as I slowly recovered, I sat in a chair, my eyes half open, my skin pale like a dead man's. I felt lost in despair, wondering if death would be better than living in this miserable world. At one point, I even thought about confessing to the crime, even though I was more innocent than poor Justine had been. While I was lost in these dark thoughts, the door opened, and Mr. Kirwin walked in. His face showed sympathy as he pulled up a chair and spoke to me in French.

"I imagine this place is awful for you. Is there anything I can do to make you more comfortable?"

"Thank you, but nothing you do will matter to me. There is no comfort for me anywhere in this world."

"I know a stranger's sympathy might not help much when you're going through something so terrible. But I believe you won't be here much longer. There must be evidence that will prove you're not guilty."

"That's not even on my mind. After everything that has happened, I am the most miserable person alive. With all the pain I've suffered, would death even be a bad thing for me?"

"These recent events have been incredibly tragic. You ended up here by some strange accident, in a land known for its kindness, yet you were immediately arrested and accused of murder. The first thing you saw was your friend's body, placed in your path as if by some evil force."

As Mr. Kirwin spoke, despite my suffering, I was surprised by how much he seemed to know about my situation. I guess my face showed my confusion because he quickly explained.

"When you fell ill, the guards brought me all the papers you had with you. I went through them to find a way to contact your family and tell them what happened. I found several letters, including one from your father. I wrote to Geneva right away. That was nearly two months ago. But you're still weak—you're trembling even now. This is not the time for any more distress."

"This waiting is worse than anything else. Tell me what horrible thing has happened now. Whose death am I supposed to mourn this time?"

"Your family is perfectly fine," Mr. Kirwin said gently. "And someone—a friend—has come to see you."

I don't know why, but my mind instantly jumped to the idea that the real murderer had come to mock me and push me toward his horrible demands again. I covered my eyes and cried out in pain,

"Oh! Keep him away! I can't see him—please, don't let him come in!"

Mr. Kirwin looked at me with concern. He thought my reaction meant I was guilty and said, with a bit of sternness,

"I would have expected you to be glad to see your visitor instead of reacting like this."

"My father!" I gasped. Every muscle in my body relaxed as relief washed over me. "Is my father really here? How kind of him! But where is he? Why isn't he here already?"

Mr. Kirwin seemed surprised—and pleased—by my sudden change in attitude. Maybe he thought my earlier outburst was just a moment of confusion. His kindness returned, and he left the room with my nurse. A moment later, my father walked in.

At that moment, nothing could have made me happier than seeing my father. I reached out my hand and asked,

"Are you safe? And what about Elizabeth and Ernest?"

My father reassured me that they were all well. He tried to lift my spirits by talking about them, knowing how much they meant to me. But a prison is no place for happiness. He looked around at the cold, bleak room with its barred windows and sighed.

"What a terrible place for you to be living, my son," he said sadly. "You left home in search of happiness, but bad luck seems to follow you everywhere. And poor Clerval—"

Hearing my friend's name was too much for me in my weakened state. I couldn't hold back my tears.

"Yes, Father," I replied. "Some horrible fate hangs over me, and I must live to see it through. Otherwise, I would have died beside Henry's coffin."

We weren't allowed to talk for long because I was still too weak, and any stress could be dangerous. Mr. Kirwin came in and insisted that I rest. But my father's presence was like a guardian angel's, and slowly, I started to recover.

As my body healed, my mind sank into deep, unshakable sadness. The image of Clerval, pale and lifeless, haunted me constantly. My thoughts became so overwhelming that my friends feared I would fall sick again. Why had they saved me when my life had become so unbearable? Maybe I was meant to live only to fulfill this terrible fate. Soon, death would come and end my suffering. When justice finally caught up with me, I would finally rest. But for now, death still seemed far away, even though I wished for it constantly. I often sat for hours, silent and unmoving, hoping for some great disaster to destroy both me and the monster I had created.

As the time for my trial approached, I had already spent three months in prison. Even though I was still weak and at risk of falling ill again, I was forced to travel nearly a hundred miles to the town where the court was held. Mr. Kirwin took care of gathering witnesses and organizing my defense. Thankfully, I didn't have to face the shame of standing in a public courtroom because the case wasn't taken to the highest court. The grand jury dismissed the charges after proof was given that I had been on the Orkney Islands when Henry's body was discovered. Two weeks later, I was released from prison.

My father was overjoyed. I was free, no longer treated like a criminal, and allowed to return home. But I couldn't share in his happiness. Whether in a prison cell or a palace, everything felt the same to me—lifeless and empty. My future was ruined forever. Even as the sun shone over me, as it did for the joyful and carefree, I saw only darkness. The only things that pierced through it were the memories of two haunting eyes. Sometimes, they were Henry's—his lifeless face framed by long dark lashes, his eyes barely visible under heavy eyelids. Other times, they were the cold, soulless eyes of the monster, just as I had first seen them in my room at Ingolstadt.

My father tried to comfort me, reminding me of Geneva and the loved ones waiting for me. He spoke of Elizabeth and Ernest, but his words only made me groan in pain. There were moments when I longed for happiness again, when I thought of my dear cousin with a bittersweet sadness. I sometimes wished to see the blue waters of the lake and the rushing Rhone River that had been part of my childhood. But most of the time, I felt numb. A prison cell and the most beautiful place on earth were the same to me. I rarely broke out of this state, except in moments of unbearable anguish. In those times, I thought about ending my own life, and only constant supervision kept me from doing something terrible.

Yet, there was one thing that kept me from giving up completely. I had a duty to return to Geneva—to protect the people I loved and to find the monster. If I ever got the chance to face him again, I would not hesitate. I would end the miserable creature's life, the being I had foolishly given a soul even more monstrous than its form.

My father wanted to delay our departure, worried that I was too weak to handle the journey. And he was right—I was nothing but a shadow of a man, a walking skeleton. Day and night, a fever burned through me. But I was desperate to leave Ireland, so he finally agreed.

We boarded a ship headed for Havre-de-Grace and set sail with the wind in our favor. It was midnight. I lay on the deck, staring up at the stars, listening to the waves crash against the boat. The darkness that swallowed Ireland gave me relief. My heart pounded with feverish excitement, knowing I would soon see Geneva. The past felt like a horrible nightmare, yet the rocking of the ship and the endless sea reminded me that this was real—Henry was gone, killed because of me and the creature I had created.

Memories rushed through my mind. I saw my childhood in Geneva, my mother's death, and my departure for Ingolstadt. I shivered as I remembered the reckless obsession that led me to create the monster. I thought back to the night it first came to life, but the memory was too painful to continue. Overwhelmed, I broke down in tears.

Ever since recovering from my illness, I had been taking a small dose of laudanum each night to help me sleep. That night, weighed down by sorrow, I took twice my usual amount and quickly fell into a deep slumber. But sleep didn't free me from my misery. My dreams tormented me, filling my mind with terrifying images.

As morning approached, I felt trapped in a nightmare. I imagined the monster's hands tightening around my throat, and I struggled, unable to break free. I heard groans and cries echoing around me. My father, who had been watching over me, noticed my distress and woke me. I opened my eyes to see the waves rolling around us, the cloudy sky above. The monster wasn't there.

For a brief moment, I felt a strange sense of peace. The present moment gave me a temporary escape from the inevitable horror of the future. The human mind, by its nature, clings to any moment of relief, no matter how fleeting.

Chapter 22

Our journey came to an end, and we arrived in Paris. I soon realized that I had pushed myself too hard and needed to rest before continuing. My father cared for me tirelessly, but he didn't understand the true cause of my suffering. He tried to help in ways that couldn't possibly ease my pain. He encouraged me to spend time with others, thinking it would lift my spirits. But I wanted nothing to do with people—not because I hated them, but because I felt unworthy of their company. They were my fellow human beings, yet I had unleashed a creature among them that thrived on their pain and suffering. If they knew what I had done, they would despise me and drive me away.

Eventually, my father accepted that I didn't want to be around others. Instead, he tried to reason with me, believing I was ashamed of being accused of murder. He told me that my pride was misplaced.

"Oh, Father," I said, "you don't understand me at all. If I felt pride, it would be disgraceful. Justine was as innocent as I am, yet she was accused of murder and executed for it. And it was my fault—I am the reason she died. William, Justine, Henry... they all lost their lives because of me."

During my time in prison, my father had heard me say similar things before. Sometimes, he seemed to want an explanation, but other times, he dismissed my words as the ramblings of a sick mind. He believed that my illness had planted strange ideas in my head. I avoided explaining myself. If I told the truth, everyone would think I had lost my sanity. But more than that, I couldn't bring myself to reveal my terrible secret—it would only fill my father with horror and fear. I desperately wanted to confide in someone, yet I kept silent. Even so, every now and then, I couldn't hold back and blurted out words like the ones I had just spoken. Though I never explained myself, speaking even a little of the truth gave me some relief.

This time, my father looked at me with shock and disbelief. "Victor, what has gotten into you? I beg you, never say such things again."

"I am not mad!" I cried. "The sun and the sky have watched me—they know the truth. I am responsible for the deaths of innocent people. I would have gladly given my own life to save them, but I couldn't. I had no choice, Father—I could not sacrifice all of humanity."

After hearing this, my father was convinced that I was not thinking clearly. He quickly changed the subject, trying to steer my thoughts away from what had happened in Ireland. He never spoke of those events again and refused to let me bring them up.

As time passed, I became calmer. The misery in my heart never faded, but I stopped speaking so wildly about my guilt. I forced myself to stay quiet, even when the urge to confess overwhelmed me. I kept my emotions under control more than I had since my terrible journey to the icy mountains.

A few days before we were set to leave Paris for Switzerland, I received a letter from Elizabeth:

My dear friend,

I was so happy to receive a letter from my uncle, saying you were in Paris. You are no longer so far away, and I hope to see you in less than two weeks. My poor cousin, you must have suffered so much! I imagine you look even worse than when you left Geneva. This winter has been unbearable for me. I've spent it in constant worry, hoping for news. But now, I just wish to see peace on your face and know that you have found at least a little comfort.

Still, I fear that the feelings that made you so unhappy last year are still there—maybe even stronger now. I don't want to trouble you at such a difficult time, but something my uncle said before he left made me realize I need to talk to you about something before we meet.

You might wonder, What could Elizabeth possibly need to explain? If that's truly what you think, then my questions have already been answered. But since you are far away, I don't know what's in your heart. Maybe you fear this conversation, yet at the same time, you want it. If that's the case, I can't delay this any longer. I must say what I've been wanting to tell you for so long.

Victor, you know that our families always planned for us to be married. We were raised knowing that this was our future. As children, we were close, and as we grew, we became dear friends. But just as a brother and sister can love each other deeply without wanting to marry, perhaps that is also the case for us. Please, tell me honestly—do you love someone else?

You have traveled, spent years away, and seen so much of the world. When I saw you last autumn, you were so unhappy and avoided everyone. I couldn't help but wonder if you felt trapped—if you believed you had to go through with this marriage only because of our parents' wishes, even though your heart was elsewhere. But that would be wrong.

Victor, I care about you deeply. I have always imagined us together in the future. But more than anything, I want you to be happy. If marrying me would make you miserable, then I would be miserable too. I can't bear the thought that you would feel forced into this. If your heart belongs to another, please tell me. Nothing would hurt me more than knowing I stood in the way of your happiness.

Please, don't let this letter upset you. You don't have to answer tomorrow, or the next day, or even before you return home. My uncle will update me on your health, and when we finally meet, if I see even a single smile on your face—whether because of this letter or something else—it will be enough for me.

Elizabeth Lavenza

"Geneva, May 18th, 17—"

The letter brought back a terrible memory I had almost forgotten—the monster's chilling threat: "I will be with you on your wedding night." That was my sentence, and that night would be when he planned to complete his revenge. He would do everything in his power to take away the small hope of happiness I had left. His ultimate goal was my death.

So be it. A deadly fight was inevitable. If he won, I would finally have peace, and his hold over me would be gone. But if I defeated him, I would be free. But what kind of freedom? The kind a man has after watching his loved ones murdered, his home burned, and his life destroyed—left wandering the world alone, with nothing. That would be my fate, except that I still had Elizabeth. Yet even her love could not erase the guilt and horror that would follow me to my grave.

Sweet, beloved Elizabeth! I read her letter over and over, and for a moment, a tiny spark of hope whispered to me of love and happiness. But I knew better. I had already lost my chance at peace, and nothing could change that. Still, I would give my life to protect her. If the monster carried out his threat, I would die. But I wondered—would my wedding speed up my fate? Perhaps it would come a few months sooner, but if I tried to delay the marriage out of fear, the creature would surely find another, even crueler way to punish me. He had promised to come for me on my wedding night, but that didn't mean he would leave me alone in the meantime. He had already proven that when he killed Henry immediately after making his threat.

I decided then that if marrying Elizabeth would bring happiness to her and my father, I would not delay it for a single day—not even for the monster's sake.

With that thought, I wrote back to Elizabeth. My letter was calm and loving.

*"My dearest Elizabeth, I fear there is little happiness left for us in this world. But whatever joy I may still find, it will be with you. Do not let your fears trouble you. I am devoted to you, and I will do everything I can to bring you peace.

I must tell you a terrible secret—one that will fill you with horror. When you learn it, you will no longer be surprised by my misery; instead, you will wonder how I have survived at all. But I will only tell you after we are married. There must be complete trust between us, my love. Until then, I beg you not to ask me about it. Please, I know you will honor this request."*

A week after Elizabeth's letter arrived, we returned to Geneva. She greeted me with warmth and love, but I saw the sadness in her eyes as she took in my thin, sickly appearance. She had changed too. She had lost weight, and the lighthearted energy that once made her so charming was gone. Yet she was even more gentle, full of kindness and understanding—qualities that made her the perfect companion for someone as broken as I was.

The brief sense of peace I had at home didn't last. The moment I let my mind wander, I was overwhelmed by the past. Sometimes, I burned with anger, filled with uncontrollable rage. Other times, I was too lost in grief to move or speak. I sat in silence, drowning in my own despair.

Only Elizabeth could pull me out of these moments. Her soft voice could calm me when I was consumed by fury, and her kindness reminded me what it meant to be human. She cried with me and for me. When my mind cleared, she would gently try to comfort me, urging me to accept what had happened. But I knew that while the suffering of the innocent could be eased with time, the guilt of the guilty never fades. Regret poisoned even the small relief I could have found in grieving.

Not long after my return, my father brought up my marriage to Elizabeth. I said nothing.

"Do you love someone else?" he asked.

"No," I replied. "There is no one else. I love Elizabeth, and I look forward to our wedding. Set the date, and on that day, I will devote myself to her—whether in life or in death."

"My son, don't speak like that," he said gently. "Yes, we have suffered great losses, but that only means we must hold on tighter to those we still have. We may be a small family now, but we will be united by love and shared sorrow. And one day, when time has softened your pain, you will find new reasons to live, new joys to heal the wounds of the past."

My father's words were kind, but my thoughts were elsewhere. The monster's threat echoed in my mind. He had never failed in his violent promises before. I almost saw him as unstoppable, and when he had sworn to be with me on my wedding night, I believed it was fate.

Still, I wasn't afraid of death—not if Elizabeth was safe. So, I forced myself to smile, hiding my fear. I agreed that if Elizabeth was willing, we would be married in ten days. In my mind, this was the final step, the moment when I sealed my fate.

Oh, God! If I had only realized what the monster truly intended, I would have left everything behind and spent the rest of my life wandering the earth rather than go through with this doomed marriage. But I was blind. Somehow, he had tricked me into thinking I was only sealing my own death. I never imagined that by setting this date, I was actually dooming someone far more precious than myself.

As the wedding day approached, I felt a growing sense of dread. Was it fear? A terrible instinct? I couldn't tell. But deep inside, my heart felt heavier with each passing day. Still, I hid my unease. I smiled, pretending to be cheerful, which brought comfort to my father. But Elizabeth was not so easily fooled.

She looked forward to our marriage with quiet happiness, but I could sense her uncertainty. The pain of the past had made her cautious—she feared that this happiness, so close and within reach, might suddenly vanish like a dream, leaving nothing behind but regret.

Preparations for the wedding were in full swing, and many people came by to offer their congratulations. Everything seemed joyful and bright. I kept my growing anxiety locked inside, pretending to be involved in my father's excited plans, even though to me, they felt more like decorations for a tragedy.

Thanks to my father's efforts, part of Elizabeth's inheritance had been returned to her by the Austrian government. Among her possessions was a small estate by the shores of Lake Como. It was decided that after our wedding, we would travel to Villa Lavenza and spend the beginning of our married life in its peaceful beauty.

At the same time, I took every precaution to protect myself in case the monster decided to attack me directly. I carried pistols and a dagger at all times and remained constantly alert to any possible trickery. Doing this gave me a small sense of control and calm. As the wedding day drew near, the creature's threat started to seem less real—almost like a bad dream that wasn't worth fearing anymore. Meanwhile, the thought of the happiness that awaited me with Elizabeth felt more certain, especially as our wedding day was discussed as if nothing could possibly go wrong.

Elizabeth seemed happy, and my outward calm reassured her. But on the very day that was supposed to bring us happiness, I noticed a sadness in her. She seemed uneasy, as if she sensed something terrible was coming. Perhaps she was also thinking about the dark secret I had promised to tell her after we were married. My father, on the other hand, was full of joy and, caught up in the excitement of the preparations, believed Elizabeth's mood was just natural nervousness.

After the ceremony, there was a large gathering at my father's house. But as planned, Elizabeth and I were to begin our journey immediately, traveling by boat and spending our first night as a married couple in Evian. The day was beautiful, the wind was in our favor, and everything seemed perfect as we set sail.

Those were the last moments of my life in which I felt happiness.

Our boat glided quickly over the water. The sun was bright, but we were shaded under a canopy as we admired the breathtaking scenery. On one side of the lake, we saw Mont Salêve, the lovely shores of Montalègre, and in the distance, Mont Blanc towering above all, surrounded by snow-covered peaks that tried in vain to match its majesty. On the other side, the Jura mountains rose dark and strong, forming an unbreakable barrier against any who wished to cross.

I took Elizabeth's hand. "You seem troubled, my love. If only you knew what I have suffered and what still awaits me... Please, let me enjoy this one day of peace, free from fear and despair."

"Be happy, Victor," she replied gently. "I don't want you to be troubled. If I don't seem full of joy, know that my heart is at peace. Something inside me warns me not to put too much faith in the happiness that seems so close, but I won't listen to that dark thought. Look at how fast we're moving! See how the clouds shift over Mont Blanc, sometimes covering its peak, sometimes lifting to reveal its beauty. Look at the countless fish swimming beneath us in the crystal-clear water, where every pebble at the bottom is visible. What a perfect day! Everything in nature seems so calm and joyful."

She was trying to lift both our spirits, to distract us from any dark thoughts. For a few moments, her eyes sparkled with happiness, but again and again, the joy would fade, replaced by quiet distraction.

As the sun lowered in the sky, we passed the Drance River and watched it carve its way through the mountain valleys. The Alps drew closer to the lake, and soon, we approached the breathtaking circle of mountains that enclosed the eastern edge. Ahead of us, we saw the spire of Evian gleaming between the trees, with towering mountains layered behind it.

At sunset, the strong wind that had carried us forward softened into a gentle breeze. The air stirred the water just enough to create a pleasant ripple, and as we neared the shore, the wind carried the fresh scents of flowers and hay toward us. The sun disappeared beneath the horizon as we stepped onto land. The moment my feet touched the ground, the fears I had tried to push away came rushing back, wrapping around me like a grip that would never let go.

Chapter 23

It was eight o'clock when we arrived. We walked along the shore for a short time, enjoying the last traces of daylight before heading to the inn. From our window, we could still make out the dark shapes of the mountains, trees, and water, even as night settled over them.

The wind, which had been calm, suddenly grew strong, now blowing fiercely from the west. The moon had reached its highest point and was beginning to sink, but fast-moving clouds rushed past it, darkening its glow. The lake mirrored the restless sky, its surface growing rough as waves began to form. Then, without warning, heavy rain started to fall.

I had stayed calm throughout the day, but as darkness swallowed the landscape, my fears returned in full force. I was tense and alert, my hand gripping the pistol hidden beneath my coat. Every small sound made my heart race. But I was determined—I would not go down without a fight. If the monster came for me, I would defend myself with everything I had.

Elizabeth had been watching me for a while, her face full of concern. At last, in a trembling voice, she asked, "Victor, what's wrong? What are you afraid of?"

I forced a smile. "Nothing, my love. After tonight, everything will be fine. But this night… this night is terrible."

An hour passed in this uneasy state. Then, suddenly, I realized something—if the fight I was expecting happened, Elizabeth would be caught in the middle of it. The thought of her witnessing such horror terrified me, and I begged her to go to our room while I stayed behind to make sure we were safe.

She left, and I spent some time pacing the halls of the inn, checking every shadowed corner, searching for any sign of my enemy. But I found nothing. For a brief moment, I allowed myself to believe that maybe, by some miracle, the monster had changed his mind or abandoned his plan.

Then, I heard it.

A scream. A terrible, high-pitched scream.

It came from Elizabeth's room.

At that instant, everything became clear. My arms fell to my sides, my body froze, and I could feel my own blood slowly pulsing through my veins. But the scream came again, snapping me out of my shock, and I ran.

Oh, God! Why did I not die in that moment? Why am I still here to relive the horror of what I saw?

Elizabeth lay across the bed, motionless and pale. Her head hung lifelessly, her soft features twisted in death, her hair falling partly over her face. No matter where I turn, I can still see her—the way her bloodless arms and lifeless body were left there, as if she had been tossed aside. How could I look upon this and still go on living? But life is cruel—it clings to us, even when we no longer want it. I only lost consciousness for a brief moment before collapsing to the ground.

When I woke up, the people from the inn were gathered around me. Their faces were filled with fear and horror, but to me, their terror meant nothing. It was just a shadow of the agony I felt inside. I pushed past them, desperate to see Elizabeth again.

She had been moved slightly, now resting with her head on her arm, a handkerchief draped across her neck and face. If I hadn't known the truth, I could have believed she was only sleeping. I ran to her and held her close, clinging to her as if I could somehow bring her back. But the moment I touched her, the awful truth sank in—her body was cold, her limbs lifeless. She was gone. And there, on her neck, was the mark of the monster's hand, proof that he had stolen her last breath.

As I hung over her, drowning in despair, something made me look up. The room had been dark before, but now a pale, eerie light stretched across it. The shutters had been thrown open, and in the window stood a figure—the one I hated most in this world.

The monster.

A wicked grin twisted his face, and with one bony finger, he pointed at Elizabeth's lifeless body. He was mocking me.

Fury boiled inside me. I grabbed my pistol and fired, but the creature was too fast. He leapt from the window, landing below with impossible speed, then ran toward the lake. Before I could react, he disappeared into the water.

The sound of my gunshot brought a crowd rushing into the room. I pointed to the spot where the monster had vanished, and a group of us took boats out onto the lake. We cast nets and searched for hours, but it was hopeless. Most of the men with me believed I had imagined him—that grief and exhaustion had made me see things that weren't real. When we returned to shore, search parties spread out into the surrounding woods and vineyards, but I already knew they would find nothing.

I tried to join them, but my body gave out. My head spun, my legs felt weak, and I stumbled forward like a drunken man before finally collapsing. Everything blurred—my vision darkened, my skin burned with fever, and I lost all sense of time. I was carried back inside and placed on a bed, but my mind refused to rest. My eyes searched the room as if I had lost something I would never find again.

After some time, I forced myself up, my body moving on instinct. I had only one thought—I had to see her.

I found Elizabeth's body surrounded by women weeping over her. I knelt beside her and added my own tears to theirs. My mind was a mess, unable to focus on any one thought. Memories of my past sorrows blurred together. William's murder. Justine's execution. Henry's death. And now, Elizabeth.

Even then, I couldn't be sure that my remaining loved ones were safe. My father—was he suffering the same fate at that very moment? Was my brother Ernest already lying dead at the feet of this monster? The thought sent a chill through me, snapping me back to reality.

I had to act. I had to return to Geneva as fast as possible.

There were no horses available, so I had no choice but to travel by boat. But the wind was against me, and rain poured heavily from the sky. Still, it was early morning, and I could reach home by nightfall if I hurried. I hired men to row, and at first, I took an oar myself, hoping that physical effort would distract me from my torment.

But I was too broken. My grief was overwhelming, and the storm inside my mind was stronger than any storm outside. I let go of the oar, buried my face in my hands, and let the darkness consume me.

Whenever I lifted my eyes, I saw places I had once known—places I had looked upon with happiness only the day before. But now, they were nothing more than cruel reminders of what I had lost.

Tears streamed down my face.

The rain stopped for a brief moment, and I saw fish darting beneath the water, just as they had when Elizabeth had pointed them out. Only hours ago, we had watched them together. But now... she was gone.

Nothing is more painful than a sudden, irreversible change.

The world around me was the same—the sun would rise and fall, the clouds would shift in the sky, the lake would carry on as it always had. But for me, nothing would ever be the same.

The monster had stolen everything.

No one had ever suffered as I did in that moment. No other person in history had ever felt such misery. My future, my happiness—everything had been ripped away from me in a single, merciless instant.

Why should I go into detail about what happened after this final, crushing event? My life had been nothing but tragedy, and I had now reached its worst moment. There is little left to tell. One by one, I lost everyone I loved until I was completely alone. My strength was nearly gone, so I will only briefly recount the rest of my miserable story.

When I arrived in Geneva, my father and my brother Ernest were still alive. But the news I brought was too much for my father to bear. I can still see him—the kind, loving man who had cherished Elizabeth as if she were more than a daughter to him. She had been his greatest joy, the one person he held onto most dearly in his old age. The monster had taken her from him, just as he had taken everything from me. Cursed be the creature that caused my father such grief and sorrow in his final days!

My father could not survive the weight of all this suffering. He grew weaker each day until finally, he could no longer leave his bed. Within a few days, he died in my arms.

What happened to me after that? I don't know. I lost all awareness of the world around me. I remember only darkness and the feeling of being trapped. Sometimes, in my dreams, I wandered through beautiful fields, surrounded by the friends of my youth. But when I woke, I found myself in a prison cell.

I later learned that I had been declared insane. For months, I had been locked away, kept in isolation. Slowly, my mind became clear again, and I was released. But what was freedom to me now? I had nothing left. My life would have been meaningless—except for one thing. When my sanity returned, so did my thirst for revenge.

As I thought back on all that had happened, I saw the true cause of my suffering. The creature I had created—the monster I had set loose upon the world—was responsible for it all. My grief turned into fury. I longed to get my hands on him, to make him pay for everything he had done.

But I didn't let my rage consume me without action. I needed a way to track him down. A month after my release, I went to a judge in town and told him I had an accusation to make. I knew the identity of the one who had destroyed my family, and I demanded that every effort be made to catch the murderer.

The magistrate listened to me with kindness and patience. "I assure you, sir," he said, "I will do everything in my power to find this villain."

"I thank you," I replied. "Listen carefully to what I have to say. My story is strange, but truth itself is often stranger than fiction. It is too detailed, too connected to be dismissed as a dream. I have no reason to lie."

I spoke firmly but calmly. I had already made up my mind—I would hunt this monster until either he or I was dead. This purpose gave me a reason to keep living, at least for a little while longer. I told the magistrate my story as clearly as I could, providing dates and details without allowing myself to lose control.

At first, the magistrate seemed doubtful, but as I continued, he became more focused. At times, I saw him shudder with horror. Other times, his expression showed astonishment, and he seemed almost convinced.

When I finished, I looked him in the eye and said, "This is the creature I accuse. I call on you to do your duty as a magistrate and see that justice is served. I also hope that, as a man, your sense of morality will not let you turn away from this."

At my words, his expression changed. Up until then, he had listened as one might listen to a ghost story—half believing, half skeptical. But now that I was asking him to take official action, his doubts returned in full force. Still, he answered me gently.

"I would gladly help you in this pursuit," he said, "but the being you describe seems to have abilities beyond anything we can fight. How can we catch something that can cross frozen seas and survive in places no man could? Besides, months have passed since these crimes were committed. Who can say where he has gone or where he is hiding now?"

"I have no doubt that he remains close by," I insisted. "Even if he has taken refuge in the Alps, he can be tracked and hunted like a wild animal. But I can see it in your face—you don't believe me. You have no intention of pursuing my enemy or bringing him to justice."

My anger flared, and my eyes burned with rage. The magistrate seemed uneasy. "You are mistaken," he said. "I will do what I can, and if it is within my power to capture the creature, he will be punished for his crimes. But based on what you've told me about his strength and abilities, I fear it may be impossible. We will try, but you should prepare yourself for the likelihood of failure."

"I refuse to accept that," I said bitterly. "But it doesn't matter. Whether or not you help me, my revenge is all that remains for me. I know it is a dark desire, but it is the only thing keeping me alive. The thought that the monster still walks free, that I have let him loose on the world, fills me with a fury I cannot describe. If you will not bring him to justice, I will. I swear that I will dedicate every last breath of my life to finding and destroying him."

As I spoke, my whole body trembled with emotion. There was something wild in my expression, something fierce and unshaken, like the spirit of a warrior ready to face his fate. But to the magistrate, a man more concerned with practical matters than with vengeance or heroism, I must have looked mad. He tried to calm me, speaking to me as if I were a sick child lost in a fevered dream.

"Sir," I said angrily, "you have no idea what you are talking about. You sit there, proud in your wisdom, but you are blind to the truth."

I could not stand to hear another word. Furious and restless, I left the building, determined to find another way to act.

Chapter 24

My mind was consumed by one thought, and one thought only—revenge. It was the only thing that gave me strength, the only reason I remained steady when grief and madness threatened to destroy me. Without it, I would have lost my mind or even my life.

My first decision was to leave Geneva forever. The home I once loved, where I had been happy and surrounded by family, now felt unbearable. I gathered some money and a few small jewels that had belonged to my mother, then set off on my journey, never looking back.

And so began my endless search—one that would only end with my death. I traveled across vast lands, facing every hardship imaginable. I crossed deserts, braved wild and untamed lands, and endured hunger, exhaustion, and bitter cold. Many times, I collapsed on the ground, too weak to go on, wishing only for death. But I could not allow myself to die, not while my enemy still lived.

When I first left Geneva, I had no clear plan. I wandered aimlessly for hours, unsure of where to begin my search. Eventually, as night fell, I found myself outside the cemetery where William, Elizabeth, and my father lay buried. I entered and stood before their graves. The only sound was the wind rustling through the trees. The night was dark, and the silence was so deep that even someone who did not know my sorrow would have felt the weight of it. It was as if the spirits of the dead surrounded me, unseen but present.

At first, grief overwhelmed me. But soon, my sorrow turned to rage. They were gone, yet I still lived. And the one who had caused their deaths lived as well. If I wanted justice, I had no choice but to keep going.

I knelt on the ground, pressing my lips to the earth above their graves. With shaking hands, I made my vow.

"By the sacred ground on which I kneel, by the souls of the dead who linger near me, and by the unbearable grief in my heart, I swear: I will not rest until I have destroyed the monster who caused this suffering. If I must live, then I will live only for revenge. I call upon the spirits of the dead—help me in my task. Let this cursed creature feel the pain he has inflicted. Let him suffer as I suffer now!"

At first, I spoke with solemnity, almost believing that the spirits of my loved ones could hear me and would give me their blessing. But as I continued, my fury grew stronger, and I could hardly speak through my rage.

Then, in the stillness of the night, I heard it.

A horrible, mocking laugh.

The sound echoed through the mountains, ringing in my ears like the voices of demons from the depths of hell. For a moment, I thought I would go mad. The laughter faded, but then a voice—one I knew all too well—whispered close to my ear.

"I am satisfied, miserable wretch! You have chosen to live, and that is enough for me."

I spun around, searching for him. In a flash, the moonlight broke through the clouds, revealing his hideous form. His twisted face was stretched into a wicked grin, his eyes filled with cruel amusement.

I lunged at him, but he was too quick. He escaped my grasp and fled with inhuman speed, disappearing into the darkness.

From that moment on, I chased him. I have spent months tracking his movements, following even the smallest clues. I followed the winding path of the Rhone River, but he always remained just out of reach. I reached the Mediterranean, and by a strange twist of fate, I saw him sneak aboard a ship headed for the Black Sea. I immediately booked passage on the same vessel, but somehow, he slipped away before I could catch him.

Through the frozen lands of Tartary and Russia, I pursued him. Though he constantly evaded me, I always found traces of his path. Sometimes terrified villagers, who had glimpsed his monstrous form, would tell me which direction he had gone. Other times, the monster himself left behind signs—perhaps to mock me, or perhaps to keep me alive so that I would continue the chase.

Snow fell heavily around me, but I pressed on. I saw the prints of his massive footsteps in the white plains.

To those who have never known real suffering, who have never felt the weight of true despair, my story must be impossible to understand. Hunger, exhaustion, and the bitter cold were nothing compared to the torment in my soul. I carried my own personal hell with me wherever I went. And yet, even in my darkest moments, I felt as though some unseen force guided me forward.

At times, when I was close to collapse, food would appear in the wilderness—simple meals, like those eaten by the local villagers, but enough to keep me alive. Other times, when I was dying of thirst, the sky, which had been clear and empty, would suddenly darken just long enough to send down a few drops of rain. I do not know if these small mercies were truly given to me by the spirits I had called upon, but they kept me from falling into complete ruin.

I tried to follow rivers when I could, but the monster avoided them, knowing they were surrounded by human settlements. In the lonelier parts of the world, I rarely saw another soul. I survived by hunting wild animals, using the money I carried to trade with villagers, or sharing my food in exchange for shelter and supplies.

But this life was unbearable. The only time I felt any kind of peace was in my sleep.

Oh, blessed sleep! In my dreams, I found a happiness that no longer existed in my waking hours. Perhaps the spirits who watched over me gave me these dreams as a way to keep me strong enough to continue. Without them, I would have crumbled under the weight of my suffering.

I endured my days only because I longed for the nights. In sleep, I was reunited with those I had lost. I saw my father's kind face. I heard Elizabeth's soft, musical voice. I imagined Henry Clerval, full of life and laughter. When exhaustion weighed me down, I would convince myself that I was simply waiting for nightfall, for in my dreams, I would return to the people I loved.

How I clung to those dreams! I reached for them as if they were real, as if they could somehow bring my loved ones back to life. Sometimes, even when I was awake, I would see their faces, hear their voices, and let myself believe—just for a moment—that they still lived.

At those times, my thirst for revenge would fade. But it never disappeared completely.

I continued forward, driven by a force greater than myself. What once felt like my own personal mission now seemed like something commanded by fate itself. My desire for vengeance no longer burned with the same wild rage, but I still walked toward my enemy, as if pushed by an unseen hand.

No matter how long it took, I would not stop. I would not rest until the monster was destroyed.

I had no way of knowing what the creature was feeling as I chased him. But from time to time, he left messages carved into trees or stone, taunting me and fueling my fury.

"My reign is not over yet," he wrote in one place. "As long as you live, I have power. Follow me to the endless ice of the north, where you will suffer from the cold that does not harm me. If you are not too slow, you will find a dead hare nearby—eat and regain your strength. Come, my enemy, we will fight for our lives, but before that, you must endure many long and painful hours."

Wretched monster! Again, I swore vengeance. Again, I promised to destroy him, to make him suffer before he died. I would never stop hunting him—either he or I would perish. And when it was over, I would finally be reunited with Elizabeth and my lost loved ones, who I believed were waiting for me after this terrible journey.

As I continued north, the snow deepened, and the cold became nearly unbearable. The people of the villages hid inside their homes, only the bravest venturing out to hunt the starving animals that had left their shelters in search of food. The rivers had frozen solid, leaving me without fish—the main source of my survival.

The harsher my struggle became, the more the monster seemed to enjoy it. In another message, he warned me:

"Prepare yourself! Your suffering is only beginning. Wrap yourself in furs and gather supplies, for soon we will enter a land where your pain will match my eternal hatred."

His cruel words only strengthened my resolve. I would not fail. Calling upon heaven for strength, I pressed on. I crossed vast frozen lands until, at last, I reached the ocean. But it was nothing like the blue waters of the Mediterranean I had known. It was covered in jagged ice, its surface rough and wild, barely distinguishable from the frozen land around it.

The ancient Greeks had wept with joy when they first saw the Mediterranean, knowing their journey was at an end. I did not weep. But I knelt and, with a full heart, thanked whatever force had guided me to this place. Here, at last, I would face my enemy.

Weeks earlier, I had obtained a sled and a team of dogs, allowing me to move quickly across the snow. I wasn't sure if the monster had the same advantage, but I soon realized that after months of losing ground, I was finally catching up. By the time I reached the ocean, he was only a day ahead of me. I felt a new surge of determination—I was close. I would catch him before he could escape again.

With renewed energy, I pushed forward. In two days, I arrived at a small, desolate village by the sea. When I asked the people there if they had seen anything unusual, they quickly gave me an answer.

A terrifying creature had arrived the night before, armed with guns and pistols. His horrifying appearance had driven a family from their home in fear. He had stolen all their food and then harnessed a team of sled dogs, forcing them to pull him out onto the frozen ocean. The villagers watched as he vanished into the distance, heading toward a part of the sea where no land existed. They believed he would soon die—either by falling through the ice or freezing in the endless cold.

Hearing this, I felt a wave of despair. He had escaped once more, and now I faced an almost impossible task—a deadly journey across the frozen ocean, where few could survive. I, who had been born in a warm and gentle land, had little hope of making it through such brutal conditions.

But the thought of letting him win, of allowing him to go free, reignited my rage. My desire for revenge crashed over me like a powerful wave, drowning out my exhaustion and doubt. After resting briefly, during which I imagined the spirits of my lost loved ones urging me to keep going, I made my final preparations.

I traded my sled for one designed to handle the rough, uneven ice of the ocean. I gathered as many supplies as I could carry. Then, without hesitation, I left the land behind and set out across the frozen sea.

I don't know how many days have passed since then. The suffering I have endured is beyond words. Only the fire of vengeance burning inside me has kept me moving forward.

Enormous mountains of ice blocked my way, forcing me to find new paths. At times, I heard the deep, thunderous cracks of the shifting ice beneath me, threatening to pull me under. But each time, the cold returned, freezing the ocean solid again and allowing me to continue.

By the amount of food I had eaten, I guessed that I had been traveling for three weeks. But my hope was stretched thin. Every time I thought I was close, the goal slipped further away. I had never felt such despair.

Then, one day, after a long and grueling climb up a steep ice ridge, one of my dogs collapsed and died from exhaustion. I stood at the top, staring out over the frozen wasteland, my heart heavy with hopelessness.

But then—I saw it.

A dark shape in the distance.

I squinted against the icy wind, straining my eyes to be sure. Then, suddenly, I knew. It was a sled. And inside, a figure I recognized immediately.

The monster.

A wild cry escaped my lips. Hope rushed through me like fire, and tears filled my eyes. I wiped them away quickly, not wanting to lose sight of him for even a second. Overcome with emotion, I wept aloud.

But there was no time to waste. I removed the body of the dead dog and gave the others a generous meal to regain their strength. After an hour—though every minute of waiting tortured me—I continued my pursuit.

The sled was still in sight. I never lost it again, except for brief moments when the ice ridges blocked my view. I was gaining on him.

After nearly two days, I was close. No more than a mile separated us. My heart pounded—soon, it would be over.

But just as I was about to reach him, everything fell apart.

A deep, rumbling sound filled the air.

The ice beneath me trembled.

The sea, which had been frozen solid, suddenly cracked with a force like an earthquake. The water beneath it roared as it swelled and crashed against the breaking ice.

I pushed forward, desperate. But it was too late.

With a deafening explosion, the ice split apart completely. In an instant, a massive stretch of open water formed between me and my enemy. He was on one side, I on the other. There was no way across.

The ice floe beneath me drifted away, growing smaller with every passing moment.

I was stranded, left to die on a shrinking piece of ice, helpless as the monster escaped me once again.

For hours, I drifted on the ice, trapped in the cold, exhausted, and close to death. My dogs began to die one by one, and I felt my strength slipping away. Just when I thought I could endure no more, I spotted your ship anchored in the distance. It was a miracle—I never imagined a vessel could travel this far north. The sight filled me with hope.

Desperate to reach you, I tore apart part of my sled to create makeshift paddles. Though it took an enormous effort, I managed to steer my ice raft toward your ship. I had decided that no matter what, I would not abandon my mission. If you were traveling south, I planned to beg you for a boat so I could continue my pursuit. But instead, I found you heading north, the very direction I needed to go.

You rescued me just as I was about to collapse completely. Without your help, I would have soon died—not from fear, but because my mission was unfinished.

Oh, when will fate finally lead me to the monster so I can have the peace I long for? Or will I die before that moment comes, while he continues to live? If that happens, Walton, I beg you—swear to me that he will not escape. Promise that you will hunt him down and see justice done.

But how can I ask you to take on my burden, to endure the same suffering that has nearly destroyed me? No, I cannot be so selfish. And yet, if he comes to you—if fate delivers him into your hands—swear that he will not walk away alive. Do not let him add more innocent victims to his list of crimes.

Be warned, Walton—he is deceptive. He speaks with great skill and can twist words to his advantage. There was a time when even I was nearly fooled by his lies. But do not believe him. His soul is as monstrous as his body, full of treachery and malice. If you ever see him, do not hesitate—think of William, Justine, Clerval, Elizabeth, my father, and even me. Remember all that he has done, and then drive your sword into his heart. I will be watching from beyond, guiding your hand.

Walton, in continuation.

August 26th, 17—

Margaret, you have read this horrifying tale, and surely you must feel the same chill of terror that runs through me even now. Sometimes, Frankenstein was so overwhelmed with emotion that he could barely continue his story. At other moments, though his voice was strained and full of pain, he forced himself to go on. His eyes—once bright and full of life—shifted between fierce anger and deep sorrow, reflecting the torment inside him.

There were times when he spoke with complete control, calmly telling me about the most terrible events as though they did not shake him. But then, suddenly, his emotions would explode like a volcano—his face twisting in rage as he cursed the monster who had ruined his life.

His story was told in such a clear and honest way that it seemed impossible to doubt him. And yet, it was not just his words that convinced me of the truth. The letters from Felix and Safie that he shared with me, as well as the sighting of the creature from our ship, made it undeniable. A monster like this truly exists. I cannot deny it, though I am still in shock.

I tried to learn more from Frankenstein about how he created the creature, but he refused to speak of it.

"Are you mad, my friend?" he said. "Do you have any idea what you're asking? Would you bring another nightmare into this world? Do not make my mistake—learn from my suffering instead of adding to your own."

When Frankenstein discovered that I had been keeping a record of his story, he asked to see my notes. He carefully corrected and added to them, especially in the parts where he described his conversations with the monster.

"Since you have written down my story," he said, "I want to make sure it is recorded fully and truthfully."

And so, a week has passed while I have listened to the most incredible tale ever told. Every thought in my mind has been consumed by it, and my heart has been deeply moved by Frankenstein himself. His noble character, his kindness, and the weight of his suffering have left a deep impression on me. I wish I could comfort him, but what could I possibly say? Could I truly encourage a man so broken, so completely without hope, to continue living? No—the only peace he can find now is in death.

And yet, even in his misery, he clings to one strange comfort. When he dreams of his lost loved ones, he believes they are truly visiting him from another world, not just figments of his imagination. This belief gives a solemn and almost sacred feeling to his dreams, making them seem as real and meaningful as life itself.

But our conversations are not always about his suffering. He has a deep understanding of literature and speaks about it with remarkable intelligence. His words are powerful and full of emotion. When he tells a sorrowful story or speaks of love and kindness, I cannot help but be moved to tears.

What an extraordinary man he must have been before his downfall! Even now, in his ruined state, he carries himself with dignity and wisdom. He knows what he was meant to be, and he feels the weight of how far he has fallen.

"When I was young," he told me, "I believed I was meant for something great. My emotions were deep, but my mind was clear and focused. I was certain that I would accomplish something incredible. This belief gave me strength when others might have been crushed by hardship. I thought it would be wasteful—almost a crime—to let my talents go unused.

When I completed my work—the creation of a living, thinking being—I felt certain that I had achieved something beyond the reach of ordinary men. I did not see myself as just another scientist or dreamer. But now, looking back, I see how blind I was. What I once thought was a great achievement has led only to misery. My ambitions, my hopes—all of it is worthless now. Like the fallen angel who dared to challenge heaven, I have been cast down into an eternal hell.

Even now, I remember the passion that drove me forward. My imagination burned with possibilities, while my mind worked tirelessly to bring them to life. I felt as if I walked among the gods, filled with power and purpose. From childhood, I was raised with great expectations and limitless ambition. But look at me now! If you had known me then, my friend, you would not recognize me in this broken man before you. Once, I never let despair touch my heart. I believed I was destined for something great, carried forward by fate itself. But I have fallen, and I will never rise again."

Must I truly lose such an extraordinary man?

I have spent my life searching for a true friend—someone who would understand me, who would share my thoughts and feelings. And here, in the middle of this frozen wasteland, I have found that friend.

But I fear that I have only found him so that I may lose him.

I wish I could convince him to live, but he refuses. Nothing I say can change his mind.

"I appreciate your kindness, Walton," he said, "but when you talk about forming new friendships and finding new people to care for, do you really think anyone could ever replace those I have lost? No one could ever be to me what Clerval was, and no woman could take Elizabeth's place.

Even when friendships are not based on great admiration, the people we grow up with always hold a unique place in our hearts. They have known us since childhood, understanding parts of us that no one else ever will. They remember who we were before we changed, and their knowledge of our past allows them to judge our actions with more certainty and trust. A brother or sister, unless there has always been some deep division, would never suspect the other of betrayal. But no matter how close a later friend may be, there will always be room for doubt.

Yet my friends were not dear to me simply because of familiarity or shared memories—they were truly good, remarkable people. Wherever I go, I will always hear Elizabeth's gentle voice and Clerval's lively conversation echoing in my mind. But they are gone. And in this loneliness, there is only one thing that keeps me from giving up my life completely.

If I had some great purpose—some noble goal that could bring good to the world—then perhaps I could continue living to fulfill it.

But that is not the path left for me. I have only one task: I must hunt down and destroy the creature I created. Only then will my time on this earth be complete, and I will finally be free to die."

September 2nd

My dear sister,

I am writing to you while surrounded by danger, unsure if I will ever see England again or the dear friends I left behind. Mountains of ice surround my ship, blocking any way of escape. At any moment, they could crush the vessel completely. The brave men who agreed to follow me on this journey now look to me for guidance, but I have nothing to offer them. Our situation is terrifying, yet I refuse to let go of my courage or hope.

Still, it is a terrible thought that all these lives are at risk because of me. If we do not survive, it will be my reckless ambition that has led to our downfall.

And what about you, Margaret? What will you go through if I am lost? You would not know what happened to me, and you would spend years waiting, caught between hope and despair. The thought of your heart slowly breaking from unanswered questions is even more painful to me than my own death. But you have your husband and your beautiful children—you still have happiness in your life. May heaven bless you and keep you safe.

As for my unfortunate guest, he looks at me with deep sympathy. He tries to encourage me, speaking as though life is something still worth holding onto. He reminds me that many explorers before us have faced the same dangers and survived. Even when I struggle to believe him, his words fill me with hope.

His influence is so strong that even the sailors feel it. When he speaks, their despair fades, and for a short time, they believe we will overcome the ice as if it were nothing more than small hills in our path. He inspires them, reigniting their strength and determination.

But these moments of confidence never last. With each passing day that we remain trapped, their fear grows. I worry that soon, their hopelessness will turn into rebellion.

September 5th

Something incredible has just happened, and even though I may never be able to send you these letters, I feel compelled to write it down.

We are still trapped in the ice, surrounded by towering frozen walls that could crush our ship at any moment. The cold is unbearable, and many of my men have already lost their lives in this bleak and merciless place. Frankenstein has grown weaker each day—his eyes still burn with fever, but his body is failing. Whenever he tries to move, he quickly collapses again, as if all life is draining from him.

In my last letter, I told you of my fears that the crew might rebel. This morning, while I sat watching over Frankenstein as he lay weak and motionless, I was interrupted by a group of six sailors knocking at my cabin door. They entered and spoke to me on behalf of the rest of the crew.

Their leader explained that they had all agreed on a request that they expected me to grant. We were trapped in the ice, and they feared we might never escape. But if, by some chance, the ice did break and an open path appeared, they worried that I would insist on continuing north, leading them into even greater danger when they could instead return home. They demanded that I promise—right then and there—that if the ship became free, I would turn south immediately.

Their request troubled me. I had not lost hope of continuing our journey, and I had never even considered turning back if we were given the chance to move forward. But could I, in fairness, refuse them? I hesitated, unsure of how to respond.

Then, to my surprise, Frankenstein, who had been silent and too weak to speak, suddenly sat up. His eyes burned with intensity, and his pale face flushed with momentary strength. He turned to the men and spoke.

"What are you saying? What are you asking of your captain? Are you really so easily discouraged? Didn't you call this a great and noble expedition? And what made it noble? It wasn't because the journey was easy—it was because it was dangerous, full of challenges that tested your bravery! You were supposed to prove your strength by facing death and hardship. You were supposed to return home as heroes, as men who risked everything for the sake of knowledge and discovery.

And now, at the first real test of your courage, you want to run away? Are you really willing to be remembered as men who turned back at the first sign of difficulty? Will you return home only to be pitied as poor, shivering souls who couldn't bear the cold and ran back to their warm homes? You didn't need to come all this way just to prove that you were cowards.

No! Be men—be more than men. Stand firm in your purpose, strong as stone. This ice is not as unbreakable as you think. It will give way if you refuse to let it stop you. Do not go back with disgrace marking your names. Return as heroes—men who faced fear and conquered it, who never turned their backs on a challenge!"

His voice carried so much power and emotion that the men were completely taken aback. His words shook them. They looked at one another, but none could respond.

I spoke next, telling them to leave and think carefully about what had been said. I reassured them that I would not force them to go farther north if they truly refused, but I urged them to reflect before making their decision.

When they left, I turned back to Frankenstein, but his brief moment of strength had faded. He had sunk back into weakness, barely able to stay conscious.

I do not know how this will end. I would rather die than return home in disgrace, my mission unfinished. But I fear that I will have no choice. The crew does not care for honor or discovery, only survival.

September 7th

The decision has been made. I have agreed to return home if we survive. My dreams have been shattered—not by the impossible, but by fear and hesitation. I am going back, defeated and empty-handed. I wish I had the strength to accept this failure with patience, but I do not.

September 12th

It is over. We are on our way back to England. I have lost not only my hopes of success and glory, but also my friend. Still, I will try to describe these painful events to you, my dear sister. As I sail home, I will not let myself fall into despair.

On September 9th, the ice finally began to shift. We heard loud cracks and booming sounds like thunder as massive chunks of ice broke apart in every direction. We were in terrible danger, but there was nothing we could do except wait and hope.

My attention, however, was focused on Frankenstein, whose condition had worsened so much that he was now confined to his bed.

Behind us, the ice continued to break, forcing the ship northward. But on September 11th, a westward wind suddenly rose, pushing the ice aside and clearing a path to the south. The moment the sailors realized they were free, they erupted into cheers—loud, overwhelming shouts of joy.

The noise woke Frankenstein. Dazed and weak, he asked me what had happened.

"They are cheering," I told him, "because they are going home to England."

"Are you really turning back?"

"Yes," I sighed. "I have no choice. I can't force these men to continue against their will. I must take them home."

"Then go if you must," Frankenstein replied, "but I will not. You may abandon your mission, but mine was given to me by fate, and I cannot turn away from it. I may be weak, but I believe the forces driving my vengeance will give me the strength I need."

As he spoke, he tried to lift himself from the bed, but the effort was too much. He collapsed back down and lost consciousness.

For a long time, I feared he was gone. When he finally opened his eyes, he was struggling to breathe and too weak to speak. The ship's doctor gave him something to ease his suffering and ordered us to leave him in peace. Later, the doctor told me that my friend had only a few hours left to live.

His fate was sealed. There was nothing I could do except wait and grieve.

I sat by his bedside, watching him. His eyes were closed, and I thought he was asleep. But then, in a faint voice, he called to me and motioned for me to come closer.

"The strength I counted on is gone," he whispered. "I can feel it—I will not live much longer. And yet, my enemy still lives. Walton, do not think that, in these final moments, I am filled with the same hatred and thirst for revenge I once had. But I do not regret wishing for his death.

I have spent these last days looking back on my actions, and I do not believe I was wrong. When I created that creature, I was caught up in my passion, but I had a duty to make sure he could live a good and peaceful life. That was my responsibility. But I had a greater responsibility—to humankind. I could not allow him to have a companion. It was the right choice.

He proved himself cruel and selfish, taking the lives of innocent people, people who had love and kindness in their hearts. And now, I don't know if his thirst for destruction will ever end. He is miserable, and he makes others suffer simply because he suffers. He should not be allowed to live. It was my task to destroy him, but I have failed.

At first, I asked you to take on this burden because I was blinded by my own rage. But now, even in my last moments, I ask again—not out of hatred, but because it is the right thing to do.

And yet, I cannot ask you to abandon your home and loved ones for this cause. Now that you are returning to England, you will likely never cross paths with him. I leave the decision in your hands. My mind is clouded by death, and I do not trust myself to know what is right.

But the thought of him living on, free to do more harm, troubles me. Still, as I wait for my final breath, I feel something I have not felt in years—peace. The faces of those I have lost appear before me, and I am ready to join them.

Farewell, Walton. Seek peace in a quiet life. Do not let ambition consume you, even if it seems harmless, even if it is only the desire for knowledge and discovery. But why do I say this? My dreams were ruined, but perhaps someone else will succeed where I failed."

His voice grew weaker, and soon he could speak no more. He lay silent for half an hour, then tried to say something again but could not. Instead, he squeezed my hand gently. His eyes closed, and he let out one last breath. A faint smile crossed his lips before it faded forever.

Margaret, how can I put into words the loss of such an extraordinary man? Nothing I say will ever fully explain my sorrow. My heart is heavy with grief and disappointment, but I am heading home to England. Perhaps there, I will find some comfort.

I must stop writing—there is a sound. What could it be? It is midnight, the wind is steady, and the men on deck are silent. But there it is again—a voice, deep and rough, coming from the cabin where Frankenstein's body rests. I must go and see what it is.

Good night, my sister.

My God! What a sight I have just witnessed! My head spins as I try to take it all in. I don't know if I can even describe it, but I must. Without this final moment, my story would not be complete.

I entered the cabin where Frankenstein's body lay. Leaning over him was a figure so massive and distorted that I struggle to find words to describe it. His face was hidden behind long, unkempt hair, but I saw one enormous hand, pale and lifeless like that of a corpse.

When he heard me enter, he stopped his cries of sorrow and turned toward the window. I had never seen anything so terrifying. His face—

grotesque and unnatural—was both horrifying and pitiful. I shut my eyes for a moment, trying to gather my thoughts. I knew what I had to do. I had promised Frankenstein I would destroy this monster.

I called out to him, commanding him to stay.

He froze, staring at me in shock. Then, he turned back to the lifeless body of his creator, as if forgetting I was even there. Every movement, every expression, was filled with a mix of grief and wild rage.

"He is another of my victims!" he cried. "With his death, my crimes are complete! My miserable life is finally at its end. Oh, Frankenstein! You were selfless and noble, and now I ask for your forgiveness—but what good is my apology now? I destroyed you by taking away everyone you loved. And now you are gone. You cannot hear me. You cannot answer me."

His voice broke, and for a moment, I hesitated. I had promised to kill him, yet seeing him in this state, filled with grief and guilt, I felt a strange mix of curiosity and pity.

I stepped closer, but I could not bring myself to look at his face again. There was something so unnatural, so beyond human understanding, that it made my stomach turn. I tried to speak, but my words faded into silence.

The creature continued his wild cries of regret, speaking in broken sentences, cursing himself for what he had done.

Finally, I found the courage to speak.

"Regret means nothing now," I said. "If you had felt this guilt before you let your hatred take over, Frankenstein would still be alive."

The creature looked at me with hollow eyes.

"You think I did not suffer? You think I did not feel agony every step of the way?" he asked bitterly. He turned toward the lifeless body again. "He did not suffer as I did. Oh, not even a fraction of what I have endured! I was driven by anger, but my heart was filled with pain. Do you think the sound of Clerval's dying cries was music to my ears? Do you think I did not feel the weight of every life I took? I was created to feel love and kindness, but misery twisted me into something else. And that transformation was unbearable."

After killing Clerval, I returned to Switzerland, broken and full of grief. I felt sorry for Frankenstein, but that sorrow turned into horror. More than anything, I hated myself. But when I realized that he—who had created me and caused my unbearable suffering—still dared to hope for happiness, my pain turned into uncontrollable rage. How could he enjoy life while I was left in misery? He had cursed me with loneliness and despair, yet he sought joy in the love and companionship I could never have. That thought filled me with jealousy and fury, making me crave revenge.

I remembered my promise to him, and I swore I would fulfill it. I knew I was only bringing more pain upon myself, but I couldn't resist the hatred inside me. I despised what I had become, yet I could not stop. And when she—Elizabeth—died, I no longer felt pain. I had silenced all feelings, destroyed all guilt, and drowned in the depths of my despair. Evil became my purpose, and I accepted it. My desire for revenge consumed me completely. And now, at last, it is over. There lies my final victim.

At first, I felt sympathy for his suffering. But then I remembered Frankenstein's warnings about how persuasive he could be. As I looked at my friend's lifeless body, my anger returned.

"You wretch!" I spat. "You dare to mourn after the destruction you caused? You set the fire yourself, and now you sit among the ashes, crying over the ruins! You are nothing but a hypocrite! If Frankenstein were still alive, he would have been your target once more. You do not grieve out of guilt—you grieve because your victim is beyond your reach!"

The creature shook his head. "No, it is not like that," he said. "But I see how my actions must appear to you. I do not seek sympathy, nor do I deserve it. Once, I longed for kindness, for love, for the warmth of human connection. My heart was filled with hope that I could find a place in the world. But now, those dreams are dead. Virtue means nothing to me anymore, and happiness has turned into endless pain. What comfort could I find in the sympathy of others? I accept my suffering. And when I die, I do not care if the world curses my name.

I used to dream of goodness, of honor, of being loved despite my terrible appearance. I once believed that people would look past my face and see the soul within me. I imagined a life filled with kindness and purpose. But I was wrong. No creature has ever fallen as low as I have. No evil, no misery, no crime could ever compare to mine. When I think of all I have done, I cannot believe that I was once the same being who dreamed of beauty and goodness. But it is true—the fallen angel has become the devil.

And yet, even the devil had companions in his suffering. I have no one.

You, who call Frankenstein your friend, know of my crimes and the suffering I caused him. But did he tell you of the long, agonizing months I spent in misery, driven by emotions I could not control? While I destroyed his dreams, I never satisfied my own desires. I longed for love and acceptance, but I was always rejected. Was that fair? Am

I the only one to blame when all of humankind turned against me? Why do you not hate Felix, who drove me away with cruelty? Why do you not curse the man who tried to kill me, even when I saved his child? No, to you, they are blameless! And I—I am nothing but a monster, something to be hated and crushed underfoot. Even now, the memory of this injustice fills me with rage.

But I do not deny what I have done. I am truly wretched. I murdered the innocent, the helpless. I strangled those who never harmed me, took the lives of those who had done no wrong. I destroyed Frankenstein, a man who was once filled with love and wisdom, dragging him into endless suffering. And now he lies here, cold and lifeless.

You hate me, but your hatred is nothing compared to the way I despise myself. I look at my own hands, the hands that committed these terrible acts, and I long for the moment when they will be gone—when I will no longer exist to remember what I have done.

Do not fear that I will harm anyone else. My work is finished. No more deaths are needed to complete my story—except my own. And do not think that I will delay in ending this misery. I will leave this ship on the ice raft that carried me here. I will go to the furthest reaches of the frozen world, where no human has ever set foot. There, I will build my own funeral pyre and burn my body to ashes, so that no one will ever learn the secret of my creation and repeat this mistake.

I will die. I will no longer feel the unbearable pain that consumes me. The thirst for love that was never quenched, the agony of being unwanted—these feelings will disappear forever. My creator is dead. And when I am gone, the memory of us both will soon fade.

I will never again see the sun or the stars. I will never again feel the wind on my face. Light, sound, and feeling will all vanish. And in that emptiness, I will finally find peace.

Once, when I first saw the world in all its beauty—when I felt the warmth of summer, listened to the rustling leaves, and heard the birds singing—death would have seemed unbearable. I would have cried at the thought of leaving such a world behind. But now, death is my only escape. My crimes have stained me beyond redemption, and my guilt will never fade. Where else can I find rest, except in the grave?

Farewell. You are the last human I will ever see.

Farewell, Frankenstein! If you were still alive and still sought revenge, you would find it best fulfilled in my suffering rather than my death. But that was never what you wanted. You only wished to stop me, to prevent more suffering. If, somehow, your soul still lingers, I know you would not wish for more punishment than what I already endure.

You suffered greatly, Frankenstein—but my agony is worse. For I will carry this guilt until the moment I take my final breath."

"But soon," he cried, his voice filled with sorrow yet determination, "I will be gone, and this pain will finally end. The suffering that burns inside me will disappear forever. I will climb onto my funeral pyre and welcome the flames as they consume me. The fire will rise and then fade, and the wind will scatter my ashes into the sea. My soul will finally rest, and if I still have thoughts after death, they will not be like the ones that torment me now.

Farewell."

As he spoke, he leaped from the cabin window onto the ice raft floating beside the ship. The waves carried him away, and soon he vanished into the darkness.

Thank You for Reading

Dear Reader,

We hope this timeless classic has sparked your imagination and enriched your literary journey. Now that you've turned the final page, we want to share a vision for the future of reading—one where every classic you've ever wanted to explore is at your fingertips, in a format that best suits your life.

We'd like to invite you to gain immediate, unlimited digital & audiobook access to hundreds of the most treasured literary classics ever written—along with the option to secure deluxe paperback, hardcover & box set editions at printing cost. Together, we can spark a new global literary renaissance alongside our small, independent publishing house called "The Library of Alexandria."

Thousands of years ago, the Library of Alexandria stood as a beacon of knowledge—until it was lost to history. We aim to reignite that spirit of preservation and discovery right now, in the modern age—only this time, it's accessible to all, in every language and every format.

Picture a world where every timeless classic, novel, poem, or philosophical treatise is not only available to read but also updated for today's readers—modernized, translated into any language or dialect, and ready to enjoy in any format you choose, whether that is in an eBook, audiobook, paperback, or deluxe hardcover & box set version a printing cost.

By joining our movement to rebuild the modern Library of Alexandria, you become part of an unprecedented mission to offer:

- **Unlimited Audiobook & eBook Access to the Greatest Classics of All Time**

  Instantly explore thousands of legendary works, from Plato and Shakespeare to Jane Austen and Leo Tolstoy. All are instantly ready to read or listen to, giving you a complete literary universe at your fingertips.

- **Paperback & Deluxe Editions at Printing Costs:**

  Purchase any title in a paperback, deluxe hardbound, or deluxe boxset edition at printing costs, shipped right to your doorstep. Curate your personal library of Alexandria with editions worthy of display—crafted to last, designed to captivate, and delivered straight to your door.

- **Modern translations for Contemporary Readers in all languages and dialects**

  Discover a vast selection of classics reimagined in clear, current language—no more struggling with outdated phrases or obscure references. Next to the original versions, we aim to offer translations in as many languages and dialects as possible.

  As we continue our translation efforts and add new languages, readers everywhere can connect with these works as if they were written today. By bridging linguistic divides, you're contributing to ensuring that these timeless stories become more meaningful, accessible, and inspiring for people across the globe.

- **Your Personal Library of Alexandria:**

  Over the months and years, you'll curate a unique physical archive of classics—each volume a testament to your taste, curiosity, and love of knowledge. It's not just about owning books—it's about curating a cultural legacy you'll cherish and pass down for generations to come.

- **Join a Global Literary Renaissance:**

    Your support fuels an ongoing mission: allowing us to reinvest in offering deluxe print editions (including special boxsets) at their true cost, broaden the range of available formats and translations, and extend the reach of these works to new audiences worldwide. By joining today, you're not just preserving a legacy of masterpieces; you set in motion a powerful wave of literary accessibility.

    We are more than a publisher—we're a movement, and we can't do it alone. Your support lets us scale our mission, preserving and reimagining history's greatest works for tomorrow's readers.

Become a Torchbearer of knowledge.

Thank you for picking up this book and allowing us into your literary journey. As you turn the pages, know that you're part of something larger: a global effort to keep these stories alive, share their wisdom across borders and generations, and spark a true cultural revival for the modern era.

If this resonates with you—please consider taking the next step by visiting:

www.libraryofalexandria.com

With gratitude and a shared love of knowledge,

The Modern Library of Alexandria Team

Visit:

www.libraryofalexandria.com

Or scan the code below:

www.ingramcontent.com/pod-product-compliance
Lightning Source LLC
Chambersburg PA
CBHW011353010726
47494CB00008B/2303